I0721293

<u>The Bat</u>

A Red Grouse Tale

Leslie Garland

Published by Noble Legacy Publishing

ISBN: 978-1-911761-38-9

The Bat

"To one who has faith, no explanation is necessary. To one without faith, no explanation is possible."

St Thomas Aquinas, 13th Century.

Introduction

When Thomas told his Thursday evening story at The Red Grouse Inn, we had a larger than usual gathering. Peter and Susan had friends, Brian and Helen, staying with them and had brought them along with what we regulars decried as rash promises of an enjoyable evening! At some stage one of our guests, Brian, asked,

"So who owns the rather derelict-looking piece of land on the left of the road, just as you go into the village?"

"Ah," said Bill, "That's where the old school used to be."

"What is it with the old school?" commented Thomas, a little testily, "After goodness knows how many years with no one mentioning it, it suddenly starts cropping up in every conversation."

"Hey, steady on, Tom. Brian only asked about the land."

"I'm sorry Brian, but just a couple of days ago our new vicar was asking me about ...," and then obviously something occurred to him, as his manner softened. "No, I'll tell you later, because, even though I say so myself, the story of the old school might make a good subject for tonight's story, that is if you're all game for it."

There were general nods and murmurings of approval from those present.

"OK then. The Old School, it is. Or perhaps, I should say, The Bat, it is," said Tom. "Thanks for the idea Brian."

"Does everyone have a drink?" asked Bill.

"Good, then if everyone is sitting comfortably," said Tom, "then I'll begin."

Chapter 1

The Summer Holidays.

Tom settled back in his chair and started his tale,
"Our teacher of those days, Mrs Simpson, was a dreadful old witch; she even had a wart on her nose and a semi-reasonable beard of grey hairs on her chin. I have no idea if she had a black cat and a besom, but I wouldn't have been surprised to learn that she had. However, what we, especially the boys, all hated about her was her bony fingers. If you did anything wrong in class such as talking, or made a mistake in your work, or your handwriting wasn't quite to her approval, the old hex would walk up to where you were sitting and commence to tell you of the error of your ways while at the same time emphasising this by drilling a bony finger into your arm, or bouncing an equally bony knuckle off your head. After an hour or two with her you went home black and blue. We boys got it worse than the girls, primarily, I am sure, because our handwriting was worse than theirs. The content of essays or correctness of answers didn't appear to matter a jot; it was the neatness of the handwriting that was important. Flowing, flowery letters, all at the same height and all slanted at the same angle, with long curling, swirling tails scored well. So all the boys in my class, including myself, didn't stand a chance. Oh goodness me, I can still remember it like yesterday; you see, I didn't get very good marks!

Much to my mother's disappointment and disapproval, my two best friends of those days were the Thompson twins, Edward (Teddy) and Robert (Bobby). Although they were twins, they were very different, as twins sometimes can be. I suppose I was more friendly with Teddy. He was much more light-hearted and carefree than his more serious brother and could (and did) get on with everyone and anyone. You couldn't dislike

Teddy. He was game for anything and everything, and would happily jump into things with both feet and if whatever-it-was did go a bit pear-shaped, he always seemed to be able to either avoid getting caught or wriggle his way out.

His brother, Bobby, who was a slightly stockier version of Teddy to look at, was not quite as outgoing; but then who could be? However, he certainly made up for that in brain power. He was one of those people who, once they had read something or been told something, just knew it. Unlike the rest of us, he didn't have to work at learning, or revise before exams; he just absorbed knowledge like a sponge, and not only that, he could also recall it from memory almost instantaneously. I always imagined that he would become the chairman of some multinational organisation and be able to run the whole thing just about single-handedly.

So, Teddy was not the brightest of the two brothers, however, he was still pretty sharp and whereas Bobby was invariably top of the class, Teddy was usually in the top five. Similarly, whereas Bobby wasn't as impulsive as Teddy, but let's face it, if you think about possibilities, options, potential escape plans and so on before jumping in, then you are not going to be as impulsive. However, he was still up for just about everything that had a bit of fun and/or adventure attached to it. And it was the Thompson twins attraction to fun and adventure that appealed to me and did not appeal to my mother.

"They're always up to no good, those two; and if you go mixing with them, Thomas, you'll end up the same way. You mark my words! Why can't you find yourself some nice, normal friends?"

Normal? I assumed by that my mother meant boring. Yes, the Thompsons certainly got up to what is generally described as 'no good', but they definitely weren't bad kids. They liked pushing the boundaries and I think they just found the humdrum nature of valley life boring and so got up to stunts and pranks just to liven things up a bit. They and I got on well together - I'll tell you how that came to pass in a minute - and we three had some good times.

Following the end of that particular term and, at last, out of the clutches of the old witch, we had the most fabulous summer. It never rained, and the skies were forever blue. We three were out every day running wild from dawn until dusk, children of nature, children of the fields and forest, without a care in the world. We 'were in Eden, the garden of God.'[1] So very, very different to the days since then," added a suddenly pensive Tom. "Childhood passes all too quickly, and that summer, I realised later, was my last taste of it. But isn't this all too often the case; only realising that something is special after the event and not at the time? At *that* time I had not 'bitten of the apple,' and so the summer days of that year were those of innocent childhood.

One passion of ours in those days was butterfly collecting; careening through long grass with a home-made net attached to a bamboo cane, trying to catch some of nature's beautiful insects in order to kill them and add them to our collections. Yes, kill them, just to add to a collection! Oh dear." Tom then explained to those of us who hadn't come across an insect killing jar, that it consisted of a galvanised metal cylinder divided into two sections by a piece of zinc gauze and had a hinged lid at each end. Apparently a piece of cotton wool soaked in ammonia was placed in one end and the beautiful butterfly placed in the other. He went on to explain that when dead, the new trophy was carefully arranged on a sheet of cork, its wings held open and in place with pins, so as to display them in their full splendour. "All this had to be done fairly quickly as I recall, before rigor mortis set-in, after which you couldn't open the creature's wings.

No, we certainly were not conservationists; that came later when we'd realised what we'd been doing, realised the error of

---

[1] Ezekiel 28:13

our ways. 'But who can discern their own errors'[2] when young?" mused Tom.

He then continued, "However, in our innocence we did learn about nature, learn about the different butterflies and moths, beetles, lizards, snakes and, of course, birds as well, though we didn't go catching them! There were some days when we got up early, well before dawn, and went up into the forest to spot deer. If we were lucky, we caught them drinking by a syke (small stream), or perhaps just standing in a clearing with a newly risen, honey-coloured sun behind them and shining through a gentle mist rising from dewy grass; an almost magical, fairytale scene of sublime natural beauty. Yes, I doubt if sunrises in Eden could have been more beautiful; though perhaps that summer, as I have already suggested, we *were* still in Eden. The world was still new, was still wonderful, and we were still amazed by it. Of course, if the deer heard or smelt us, they were off, and with long easy jumps disappeared effortlessly into the trees leaving us, feeling let down, a little cheated, that all our efforts made to see them had been so suddenly dashed."

A wistful Tom then added with a chuckle,

"And talking of the forest, reminds me that it was that same summer when we built a fantastic tree house in an old oak tree. OK, it wasn't so much a house, more a platform of branches tied together with rope; rather like the raft of the wreck of the Hesperus that had been washed up on a high tide and had landed in a tree. However, the views from this aerial castle were amazing and we felt as if lords of all we could see."

Then he laughed at a further recollection which he went on to share,

"One day, Teddy Thompson fell off and landed in a hawthorn bush directly below. Perhaps needless to say, we all thought it was hilarious, though also, perhaps needless to say, Teddy

---

[2] Psalms: 19:12

didn't. For some uncharitable reason, this reminded me of the story of Brer Rabbit and the tar baby, though poor Teddy was, that day, minus one tar baby. His usual luck certainly had deserted him because, by the time he'd got out of the bush, he was full of thorn splinters. Even my mother felt sorry for him and carefully took the splinters out with a needle and a pair of tweezers."

"Sounds idyllic Tom, as long as you avoided hawthorn bushes," said Bill with a wry smile.

Tom looked at Bill and grinned before continuing,

"And you know Bill, when deer safaris, high adventure and surveying our imagined kingdom weren't on the agenda, there were those *extremely* idle and *extremely* lazy days when we went .... " and here Tom paused for effect before adding, "*fishing!*"

And oh yes, this had the desired effect, with all around the table bursting into laughter, as everyone knew how keen Bill was on fishing.

"Yes", said Tom, after the hubbub had died down, "it was lovely just lying on your back in the lush green grass of the river bank, watching the clouds go drifting by overhead like large white fluffy galleons in some aerial Armada, listening to the buzz of insects and the rustling of leaves in the trees while sharing a bottle of ginger beer. Yes, ginger beer came in bottles in those days; brown glass bottles with white china stoppers with a rubber washer, all of which were attached to the bottle, and so could be used to reseal it by twisting a bent wire contraption attached to the stopper. Occasionally, we'd see the bright blue flash of a kingfisher, or watch a white breasted dipper bobbing up and down on a rock in midstream, before flitting off, just inches above the babbling water, to alight on another rock further downstream, where, once there, would again proceed to bob up and down. Dragonflies and damselflies darted about over the water and in the open sunlit patches above the riverbank, the sunlight dancing off their iridescent, green and blue bodies. We never caught very much. Indeed, now that I come to think about it, I'm not sure if we ever caught anything. Er .... Bill will explain."

There was another chuckle from those listening, and Bill shot Tom a pointed glance, along with a smile.

"And then, on really hot days, we used to go to a stretch of the river we called 'the pool'. Here, we macho chaps indulged in splash fights, trying to duck each other and, inevitably, swimming races between a rock and a low hanging branch of an alder which had all-but fallen into the river on the downstream side."

He then went on to explain for the benefit of the two new arrivals that 'the pool' wasn't actually a pool, but was a bend in the river, just up from the village, where the river bed was gouged out every winter when the river was in spate and so was usually a good six feet deep on the outside of the bend. In the summer, of course, it flowed much more gently. On the inside of the bend, there had been, and still is, a sand bank of lovely soft sand where clothes could be left, and the Olympic athletes lie in the sun and bronze themselves.

"Occasionally, we had a barbecue on the sandbank, though these were usually group affairs with some of the girls joining us. We had no barbecue kits in those days. So old dry pieces of wood, branches and scrap wood, all of which had been collected during the previous week, were broken up and placed within a ring of stones. Once a good fire had been got going, fir cones were added so as to get it really hot and without too much smoke - it's no fun trying to cook your sausage when there's smoke blowing in your eyes," Tom informed us, before going on to explain, "I seem to recall there was a lot of serious technique applied to the fire - macho man, him light fire! - and perhaps not enough applied to the actual barbecuing, because, as I remember, invariably the odd sausage or two ended up in the glowing embers, much to the disappointment of whoever was trying to cook it and the amusement of the rest of us.”

“Ah, yes, those days were all great fun,” concluded Tom dreamily, still a little lost in his rose-tinted world of yesteryear; his recollections of his childhood Eden. “It really was a fantastic summer, indeed, an idyllic summer, and now I look back on it, very much a summer of sweet, childhood innocence.”

Chapter 2

The First Week Of The Autumn Term.

"Usually, none of us had any enthusiasm for going back to school in the autumn. However, that year was different. Mrs Simpson (The Witch) had retired at the end of the previous school year, and we were to get a new teacher, so we went back to the new term and new year with a mix of curiosity and anticipation of this new teacher. However, before I tell you about her, I had better tell you about the old school building.

The school we attended was not the one in the really old church school building which is almost opposite the church and is now the tearoom, but the one which was located on the patch of ground that Brian was enquiring about, on the left hand side of the road just as you go into the village. It was not a single building, but consisted of a number of prefabricated huts seated on brick plinths and placed close together so as to give the impression of being, if not one building, at least one unit. However, the little flights of steps leading up to each hut, or classroom, rather gave the game away that the whole thing was in fact cobbled together from separate parts.

Each hut had arrived on the back of a wagon, and was rather like a large wooden flat-pack container consisting of a floor, obviously, walls, comprised of coloured plastic, I think, infill panels to the lower sections, a rather yucky olive green as I remember, glass windows to their upper sections and a flat roof. They were cheap, in all senses of the word, were perishing cold in winter and the roofs invariably leaked somewhere. There were six of them; two rows of two, with a further two out the back and set at right angles to the other four. To us kids, they were all a bit reminiscent of the huts you see in prison camp war movies, though actually, they didn't bear much resemblance to them. Although the whole lot has gone now, you can still see roughly where they were. The old stone masonry entrance gateway from the road is still there and now forms the entrance to the field. Back in those days, this entrance led to a tarmacked area in front of the first two classrooms. Our playground area was off to the south side of the huts, remote from the village, no doubt so that the noise of our playing didn't upset the residents. Like most school kids I suppose, none of us loved the place at the time and it was referred to variously as Colditz, which, of course, was a totally inappropriate name, or Stalag Luft 111, which was perhaps a little more appropriate, given that the latter did at least contain huts in which to house its prisoners.

So, on the first day of the autumn term, at nine o'clock on a Monday morning, we were all sitting at our desks when in came Old Badger, with our new teacher.

Old Badger was the headmaster. He was also relatively new at the school, having only taken up his post twelve months previously. And why Old Badger? Well, unusually, he had a white stripe of hair on the top of his head, whereas the hair on either side still had its colour, and we thought it made him look like .... Oh, come on, we were school kids! However, it was only his hair which resulted in this nickname, because his face was most un-badger-like, being round and weather-beaten. He was one of those 'chaps' who loved competitive sports, feeling that they were good for developing a schoolboy's, and presumably a schoolgirl's character, though he was very much a man's man and actually had little clue about how to deal with the girls, relying entirely on the female members of staff to attend to that. 'Children need plenty of exercise and fresh air,' was his motto, and so probably was, 'and need to be freezing cold in the winter,' as I am sure Old Badger thoroughly approved of the school buildings' lack of both proper heating and insulation. 'We don't want pupils of this school growing up as soft good-for-nothings!' His choice of clothing admirably illustrated his lack of imagination, as he always seemed to be dressed in the same tweedy-looking jacket, trousers and waistcoat; an almost mustard coloured affair, though a bit greener than mustard, with 'schoolmaster brown leather cuffs and elbow patches' to the jacket. Beneath this he sported, though Badger wasn't really the type of man who 'sported' clothing, a white shirt and military-looking tie.

Looking back, I suppose he was a reasonable headmaster. We could have had worse. But as said, he didn't have much imagination, which is probably why he'd been put in charge of us lot. He always assumed that what seemed obvious at first glance was in fact the case, without ever mentally stepping back and analysing the situation more carefully before pronouncing on it. It ought to go without saying of course, that as often as not he got hold of the wrong end of the stick and ended up blaming the wrong kids for something they hadn't done, and then, by the time he'd realised that he'd got the wrong culprits, he'd forgotten the original evidence, and so was unable to backtrack and locate the real perpetrators of whatever dastardly deed had been done. However, he was a good front man, always standing up straight, his chest out, his military-looking tie to the fore, in front of us, or the school, or our parents, as the occasion demanded, like an archetypal sergeant major facing his troops, barracks, or visiting dignitaries.

And now to our new teacher.

Wow! She was gorgeous. After what we had been used to, any woman without a black cat and a broomstick would have been wonderful, but Louise Loveless, as we subsequently learned was her name, was a real beauty. She must have been in her early thirties, but I am guessing that now, because back then we were at the age when all adults looked old, and to be honest, we, by which I mean we boys, were not really interested in irrelevant details like her age. Surprisingly, I can still remember that on that day she wore a figure-hugging, slightly formal black skirt, which showed off her hips wonderfully, accompanied by a matching black jacket which was unbuttoned to reveal a virgin white blouse done up to the neck and stretched across a pair of the most amazing tits that I had ever seen. Her face was rather on the pale side, which enhanced her full cupid's-bow, red lips, which were set beneath a rather long nose, and blue-green, sultry and hollow-looking eyes. And, most importantly, she had not the least sign of a wart or beard. Her face was surrounded by the most magnificent red hair, which tumbled over her shoulders and down her back. If I said she looked as if she had stepped straight out of a pre-Raphaelite painting, I am sure you will have a pretty good idea of what she looked like; absolutely stunning. The girls in the class thought she looked 'really beautiful' and the boys thought .... well, I am sure you can guess what the boys thought! From The Witch to Louise, talk about going from one extreme to the other.

As you can probably guess, poor Old Badger didn't manage the introductions too well, probably as a result of being more captivated by and disconcerted by her than we were. And it wasn't just ourselves and Old Badger who were disconcerted by her arrival, our parents were as well. The mums found her 'a lovely woman, oh so much better than that Mrs Simpson' and the dads found themselves concurring with their wives without any difficulty whatsoever, 'oh yes, definitely, a lovely woman!' - though perhaps not for quite the same reasons as their wives and for very much the same reasons that caused Old Badger to be so discomposed - and it was noticeable how the number of dads who found that they did *just* have time to both bring their kids to school in the mornings and collect them later in the afternoons increased quite dramatically.

Yes, eventually we did get down to our lessons, though there was no doubting that it was difficult for us boys to concentrate on Pythagoras' rule for right angled triangles, or adjectival clauses of something-or-other when faced with either those wonderful breasts bursting to get out of that tightly stretched white blouse as she addressed the class, or that lovely rounded bottom in that tight black skirt while she wrote at full stretch on the blackboard.

Chapter 3

Felicity And Louise.

Louise continued to look as lovely as ever, even after she had stopped wearing the tight black skirt and jacket, which she had dispensed with after her first week with us. She had then chosen more casual attire; a pleated skirt, which came down to just below her knees, had replaced the tight figure-hugging number, and blouses which were not done up to the collar, but had a button or two left casually undone, replaced the previous, more strict, schoolmarmish white job. It's quite amazing, isn't it," said Tom, aside to us, "how schoolboys *can* take an interest in women's clothing? But, back to my story. Presumably, our new teacher felt more relaxed in her new role and so no longer in need of dressing in such a formal and disciplinary manner. However, even if she was more relaxed, her blue-green eyes belied this, as they still looked dark and tired.

As far as we boys were concerned, there were upsides and downsides to this change in her attire. The upside was when she walked around the classroom and stopped in front of your desk and bent down to look at your work, her casually undone blouse had a tendency to fall open and goodness, what a lovely view you had. They were magnificent; full, round, pale-skinned, smooth and soft. The downside was that this wonderful treat completely put you off your work and invariably gave you a hard-on. The girls knew this and looked and pointed, and giggled behind their hands, while you sat there desperately trying to think of anything that would result in the reduction of the bulge in your trousers. Some, like Teddy Thompson, didn't care less and regularly put their hands up while she was walking around so that she would pay their desk a visit, when they would ask some inane question, just so they could get an eyeful.

The very fact that this didn't happen just by accident and on one day alone, made it eminently clear that Miss Louise wasn't entirely innocent in this. Of course she must have known what we boys were doing, but she didn't button-up and none of us got reprimanded. Oh yes, Miss Louise Loveless knew how to use her femininity, and knew the effect that she had on men and us boys. We did indeed notice that she certainly knew how to turn on a slightly flirty manner, flash an eyelid, wriggle her bottom and now we knew, flash her tits. Perhaps this was a relatively harmless method of stopping us from playing around in class? It certainly worked, because none of us boys wanted to be sent out of the room to go and stand in the corridor and we were all only to happy to call her over to get her to explain something that we hadn't quite grasped, while at the same time getting a lovely view of something that we so much wanted to, but weren't permitted to grasp! No, she didn't have any problems with class discipline.

Although Miss Lovelies, as we boys had started to call her - no guesses as to why - was our designated school teacher, I suppose you would say our class teacher, we did have other teachers for different lessons. One of these was Felicity. She also didn't have any problems with class discipline. However, she maintained it in a very different manner from Miss Loveless.

Felicity had just married Aidan Shaw at that time and so had become Mrs Felicity Shaw. She took us both for History and for Religious Instruction, otherwise known as R.I.; a somewhat strange combination, but that is how it was. She was very much a local girl, having been born in the valley, which is why we all knew her as Felicity, rather than as the more formal Mrs Shaw, which at that time we hadn't really got used to anyway. She had gone away to study and train as a teacher and had then returned to the village. She wasn't a stunning beauty, but she did have a gentle, fresh prettiness about her. However, that did not stop her from being charming, even if she was a touch reticent, some might say shy in her demeanour. She was a genuine person;

good, considerate, kind, and didn't hold a grudge, even against her most argumentative pupils. This was just as well, because she had an easy-going manner and had a tendency to run her classes more like discussion groups, rather than as formal classes with the teacher standing at the front and telling us pupils the facts. However, she could be firm and formal when the occasion demanded. Her only fault, if one can call it that, was that at times she could be a little bit prim, a little bit narrow minded and a touch too certain, especially when talking about religion and, as already said, she had us for R.I.

Unlike Old Badger, Felicity seemed to know exactly what was going on and who was up to what. You couldn't hide anything from her and so as a result no-one did for long. Her easy-going nature did not allow her to get cross, and whereas she didn't mind the odd bit of mucking about, when she thought there had been enough and that we ought to get back to learning, she would simply say the name of whoever had been pushing their luck, and ask them to explain, in detail, to the rest of the class, 'how Napoleon had won the Battle of Austerlitz', or 'what was the precise meaning behind a particular parable' in order to get them to pay attention and keep them from mentally wandering off again.

Mrs Felicity Shaw and Miss Louise Loveless didn't really get on with each other from day one. I don't recall anyone reporting any blazing rows, but there was no doubting that there was a certain frostiness between them. Perhaps it was because they were almost polar opposites in character and temperament? Possibly Felicity saw Louise as a showy and flirty hussy, and possibly Louise saw Felicity as a timid, prim, church mouse? Or perhaps it was because they were, in fact, each a little jealous of the other; Felicity with Louise's very attractive good looks and ease with which she socialised, especially with men, none of which was in her (Felicity's) nature, and Louise with Felicity's quiet efficiency and obvious contentment and happiness at being newly married, something, which she

(Louise), didn't have? However, whatever the reason, or reasons, they didn't get on and didn't spend any longer in each other's company than they had to.

Chapter 4

The Donation.

It was sometime in the first half of October when a van pulled up in the school yard and three wooden crates were delivered. Our class was given the job of unpacking these crates, much to the envy of the other classes who, of course, would also have liked to have exchanged maths or English grammar for a bit of crate opening; who wouldn't?

As I was the biggest boy in our class, Miss Loveless presented me with the jemmy and instructions to,

"Prise up the planks, Thomas, but gently, mind you."

These were then lifted off, and inside these crates were found various wooden-framed, glass-sided cases containing a variety of stuffed animals and birds, along with some large bell-jars also containing smaller stuffed specimens. As the school didn't have a library or science room, there was no obvious place to put these new treasures. So the headmaster and Miss Loveless, both of whom had been watching the proceedings, decided that the room used as a film room would have to do for the time being until something more permanent could be sorted out.

The film room was the second of the two huts at the back of the school, the one nearest the playground on the south side. It was equipped with blackout curtains and had a pull-down screen mounted on the ceiling at one end. You entered the hut at the screen end, just in front of a stud-wall, which separated a narrow store room from the main body of the hut. In this storeroom were kept writing books, pencils, the ink - yes, we still used ink in those days - blotting paper and such like. Back in the main room, there were squat towers of stacking-type, tubular steel framed, plywood-seated and backed chairs, set at intervals along the sides of the room. At the far end of the main room, various surplus desks were piled up on top of one another, though with a gap between them in the centre where a single desk stood with a purpose-made wooden box-plinth on top of it, upon which sat the cine film projector. The films for this used to arrive at the school on large spools in round tins and were usually shown after school proper had finished. They were commonly of an infrastructural or geographic nature, such as a water project in Africa, or rice cultivation in Indonesia. You get the idea. As there was no TV in those days and we had no cinema in the village, being able to see these was a bit of a treat, and many of us stayed behind after school to see a film when one was being shown.

Old Badger and Miss Loveless decided that some of the stacks of chairs would be moved to the back of the room, thus permitting desks to be arranged along the two sides of the hut and next to the windows, and the collection of stuffed, dead wildlife to be set out on these desks. We boys were given this task. Perhaps needless to say, this took us a while. The girls stood around uselessly, talking and giggling to each other, while we boys moved stacks of chairs and humped desks about. When at last the job was done, some of the girls did make themselves a little bit useful carrying in and positioning some of the smaller specimens. However, it fell to us boys yet again, to carry in the larger exhibits.

After getting my breath back, I noted it was a strange collection. You couldn't noticing that everything about it was so dreadfully old. The so-called exhibits could well have been pulled from some fusty old museum, where you might have had to brush the cobwebs away as you walked between the rows of cases. Everything about them just exuded 'ancient' and 'antiquated'. The actual wooden cases were possibly made of mahogany or some similar exotic wood, and the glass set into their sides and tops was most certainly not plate glass. It had a greenish tint to it, and as you moved your eye relative to it you could see that it was not optically correct, with a bird's beak or eye appearing larger or smaller depending on where you viewed it from. The bell-jars likewise looked as if they had come off the ark. The glass of which they were made had similar faults to the glass in the cabinets. Namely, variable thickness and a greenish tint, both of which distorted your view of the encased exhibit. All the cabinets and jars had dark mahogany bases, upon which were fixed small brass plates with the name of the incumbent inscribed on them.

And then there were the actual 'zoological specimens' themselves; the animals and birds. To say that they all looked as if they had been dead for quite a long time, was a bit of an understatement. Fur looked moth-eaten, feathers stuck out at strange angles or were missing altogether, and many of the specimens were posed at an angle at which, had they been alive, they would have fallen over! And if the presentation of these motley-looking beasts wasn't enough to drain you of any enthusiasm, the choice of specimens was also, to say the least, bizarre. There was a lopsided fox that appeared to have no fur on its snout. The brass plate on the base of its display case was inscribed 'Renard'. Had it come from France? I had no idea. There was a large owl which looked as if it had flown through a hedge backwards and, if the angle it was sitting on its branch was anything to go by, was still suffering from the effects of same! There was a magpie, also sitting on a piece of branch, and there was a Crow, though it was standing on a piece of rock, with its head forward and low, and croaking. One of the large cases contained a small goat attempting to leap, though looking as if it stood a far better chance of falling sideways through the rear of the glass case. The brass plaque on the base of this specimen proclaimed it as 'Capricornus'. And there was even a pangolin. This looked better than most of the others in the collection, probably because it had no fur or feathers to get moth-eaten or disarranged, and its shiny plated body still retained its shiny plated form. There were others, but I cannot remember them.

I do remember that in one of the not-quite circular bell-jars was a fat, flat, warty-looking toad, which had a brass plate on the base proclaiming it to be 'Bufo bufo'. Of course, we kids didn't know anything about Latin nomenclature for zoological specimens, and so thought the names on the various plaques were the given names of each; rather like the names of our two collies on the farm, Blackie and Patch. Another bell-jar contained a moth-eaten looking weasel, which had the name Mustela inscribed on its brass plate. There was an inclined Cobra snake called Naja, with its head raised and hood puffed out. As with the display cases, there were more exhibits in the bell-jars, but my memory fails me. However, I am sure you get the picture. Oh yes, and finally, and I mustn't forget this one, there was a very leathery-looking, black bat hanging from a makeshift piece of tree.

"Ooh! I wonder if it's a vampire?" enquired Marianne Cole when she saw the bat. With long straight dark hair, a pale complexion and a love of all things ghoulish, Marianne was the original goth, back before goths had even been thought about.

"No, I don't think so," answered Miss Loveless.

I could see that Teddy Thompson was paying particular interest to all of this. If there was mischief to be done, a prank to be played, or trouble to be got into, then Teddy was, as likely as not, going to be in the thick of it. I knew him well enough to realise that he had seen 'potential' here for something.

So too had his brother, Bobby, who asked, "Where shall I put this one, Miss?"

"Just put it on the desk next to you," Miss Loveless replied, only for him to deliberately set it down towards the back of the desk and at an angle, guessing that she would go over to straighten it, inevitably have to bend over the desk, thus pushing out both her bottom and bust whilst doing so. Bobby's sense of fun was, shall we say, a little more calculated than his brother's.

The next morning, in assembly, Old Badger announced in a pompous voice that the collection that we had unpacked the previous day had been donated to the school by a local benefactor with the grand-sounding, indeed almost Ruritanian-sounding name of Dr Maximillian Syphre. Apparently, we were to feel proud and grateful that our school had been favoured with this wonderful donation. I did wonder if Old Badger had actually had a close look at the various 'exhibits,' because the manner of his waxing on about them didn't quite tally with what I had seen.

Dr Maximillian Syphre, our generous benefactor, was, with a name like that, obviously not a local, though he had lived up at High Field for a good few years. Apparently, he had died just recently. Although I'd been to High Field once with my father when he'd had to deliver some lambs, I hadn't met Dr Syphre. High Field House was, as I remember it, a strange, cold, grey, stone-built Gothic pile with round towers topped with conical slate roofs. It was, indeed I suppose it still is, set in its own grounds, surrounded by trees and located in splendid isolation up on the moors in the direction of Hartstane and would have made an ideal location for filming a ghost or horror movie.

As Old Badger explained, old man Syphre had felt that these 'exhibits', or 'zoological specimens,' would be of educational use to us children. It did and still does amaze me how people think that something that they treasure, or possibly don't treasure at all and are prepared to give away for nothing, will be valued by others. If these moth-eaten relics had been mine, I would have put the lot on a bonfire. They were dreadful. However, in spite of that, there was no doubting that they were a stimulus for lessons on wildlife, adventure stories and geography, as well as ideas for pranks for Teddy Thompson. And the first of these was to suggest that one of the animals had moved as he was looking at it.

"Now we know that is not true, Edward. So don't fib; there's a good boy," said Miss Loveless.

"But it did, Miss. I lifted up the glass front and ...."

"Don't you go doing anything like that again, Edward Thompson," said Miss Loveless in a sharp tone, uncharacteristic for her, and then added in a slightly gentler tone of voice, "We know the animals and birds are dead, so they can't move. But, due to their age, they are delicate. So please, children, leave the cases closed."

But Teddy had sown a seed. A day later, one of the more sensitive girls in our class came rushing out of the room with a hysterical, 'It moved! It definitely moved! I saw it!' and had to be hugged by Miss Loveless until she calmed down, and no, she had not opened one of the cases. This claim, that of the animals moving, soon spread, and others in different classes to ours were also saying that they had seen one or more of the stuffed exhibits move.

Good one, Teddy.

Chapter 5

The Following Week.

On the Monday after Teddy had played his first prank, he told me that the case he had opened was that of the moth-eaten fox (Renard), the one with almost no fur on its snout. He then went on to tell me that on the Saturday evening, he and Bobby had come back to school when it was dark and got into the room - somehow they had obtained a key for the door from somewhere - in order to have a look round in the dark, and ....

"The fox, what's-his-name, weren't there."

"Oh, come on Teddy. You don't think I believe that, do you?"

"Honest, Tom. It weren't there."

"Do you really think I am as daft as Sheila Simonds?"

Tom then explained that Sheila Simonds was the silly, hysterical one who'd had to be hugged by Miss Loveless. After this explanation, he continued,

"No, Tom. But I'm telling you. It weren't there!" said Teddy.

Now, perhaps I need to explain why Teddy, Bobby and I got on so well together. When we had been in the second year the three of us had been in the vicarage garden scrumping apples one day, and the vicar, a limp fish called Bitterling, the Reverend Bitterling, nearly caught us. Teddy and Bobby obviously either weren't recognisable at a distance, or were faster at their getaway than I was. Anyway, I got identified and called in by the then headmaster, the one before Old Badger. He then gave me the 'third degree' vis-a-vis who else was involved. Although I was pretty sure he knew the Thompsons were there in the vicarage garden with me, he couldn't prove it. I stuck to my story that I was on my own and got my backside tanned for my sins, but presumably because I hadn't split on the Thompsons and had suffered for it, thereinafter I had the confidence of both of them.

Looking back on that incident, I have since wondered if that was when I first started to gain knowledge. Bitterling's apple tasted sweet, but was it because it was a sweet apple or was it because it was a stolen one; an illicit pleasure tasting the sweeter because it was illicit? Or, as I subsequently learned, was the pleasure gained solely from participating in the act of theft; 'Could I enjoy doing wrong for no other reason than that it was wrong?' as St Augustine had posited.[3] So is the allegory of Adam and Eve eating of the Tree of Knowledge, not so much about gaining knowledge by eating the fruit - the apple containing some elixir which jolted their brains into action - but by the very act of *taking* the fruit, the theft, the act of doing something that was forbidden, the breaking of the rules, the in-effect-saying, I will go my own way, make my own choices? To not take of The Tree and to accept the status quo, would be to remain as a child. Yes, life would be easier, more akin to that in Eden, but would such a life, where the individual had never dared to take responsibility for the course of it, a life in which all the real decisions had been made by others, all the rules been set by others, be as satisfying as one that the individual had carved out for themselves?

To a greater or lesser extent, don't we all follow the easy path? We go to school because the law, a rule set by the state, says we have to. While there, we follow the rules of the school. We take our exams, jumping through sets of hoops like trained dogs in order to get a piece of paper which categorises us, defines whether we are a square pin or a round one in the particular subject in question. And then, we take this piece of paper and go and get a job, and do as our employer tells us, for which they give us a pay cheque at the end of the week, or month. All the

---

[3] St Augustine, Confessions, Book II

way along, we have lived by the rules set by others - 'Now these are the commandments, the statutes, and the judgments,'[4] - and so we are, perhaps more than we realise it, still in The Garden and have still not dared to touch The Tree. Those of us who are a little more daring and do approach The Tree, and have a little nibble of the fruit, unfortunately do not find that, as the serpent suggested, 'then your eyes shall be opened, and ye shall be as gods,'[5] which is a bit of a shame! But continue to have to follow most of the rules, though, as a result of that little bit of a nibble, it is possible to leave one or two of them behind.

But, back to where we were with Teddy.

There was no reason for Teddy to have told me anything about this latest exploit of theirs; they hadn't been caught and weren't looking for an alibi, or similar. Getting into the school at night could have just remained their secret. It goes without saying, I trust, that I knew both Teddy and Bobby well enough to know that they could swear to tell the truth, the whole truth and nothing but the truth, and, if you required it, swear on their grandmother's grave as well, that they were telling the truth, and then look you straight in the eye and lie through their teeth! But what reason had Teddy to lie to me? Indeed, why was he even telling me this when he didn't need to? And why was he telling me now, several days after the event?

I reckoned that he'd probably been thinking about it and had decided that he needed to tell someone, and so I concluded that perhaps, just perhaps, his story was true and that possibly, just possibly, Teddy was a little frightened? Yes, both seemed highly unlikely, as usually Teddy wasn't afraid of anything, but what else could be prompting him to tell me this? And then, no sooner had Teddy finished telling me of this improbable incident than we (he and I) learnt from Dave Parker that his father's chicken run had been raided over the weekend and that he'd lost almost

---

[4] Deuteronomy 6
[5] Genesis 3:5

all of his birds.

"You see Tom," said Teddy as soon as we were out of earshot of Dave Parker, "I told you that it had gone," he immediately assuming that it was moth-eaten Renard that had raided Dave Parker's dad's chicken run.

"A long dead-and-suffed fox doesn't go raiding chicken runs," I pointed out, and then, as I confess I was curious about Teddy's story, added as a bit of an after-thought, "Have you still got the key to the door?"

Although we were not allowed into the school during playtimes, it had occurred to me that if we could get into the classroom containing the exhibits, it would be easy to check if the fox was still there, as of course I expected it to be.

"Yeah, here," he said, pulling it out of his pocket.

We made our way over to the film-room hut and then, like two archetypal shady crooks, with our backs and palms of our hands against the wall, edged our way round to the end of it.

"We can't both go in. Someone will have to stand guard to signal if the coast is clear when whoever does go in is ready to come out."

"I'll go in," volunteered Teddy, game as ever.

"No, Teddy, I'll go," I said firmly, as I wanted to see this for myself. "I'll tap on the door when I'm finished. You tap back if the coast is clear."

And with that, I went quickly up the steps, opened the door, went in and closed the door again behind me. Almost straight away, I could see that the fox was alive and well and in his box, if that doesn't sound like a totally stupid way to describe a dead, stuffed fox in a display case? As I could see dear old Renard almost from the door, I didn't go over to his case to make a more thorough check on him - yes, he was there, that was all I needed to know - before going back to the hut door and tapping it.

"But honestly, Tom." said Teddy, when I'd rejoined him outside and we were back round at the end of the hut and I had him up against its end wall, and was threatening to punch his head, "It weren't there when we went back that evening. The case was empty."

Yes, as I have already said, I knew Teddy could lie the hind leg off a donkey, but as I've also already mentioned, although this was Teddy telling me this, I was partly inclined to believe him simply because there was no reason for him to lie to me, or indeed for him to have told me anything in the first place. However, in spite of my well-considered and logical reasoning, I couldn't be one hundred percent certain; it was Teddy who was telling me this after all.

Later on in the afternoon Miss Lovelies announced that we would have a film show; not a movie-type film show, but some slides. She produced a slide projector and some Kodachrome transparencies, and we all filed along to the film-room, though that name was probably no longer appropriate, and 'museum-room' was now perhaps more apt? Once inside, we all dashed off to look at the moth-eaten exhibits.

"Jennifer! I told you not to touch the cases," snapped Miss Loveless somewhat unnecessarily, as it appeared that all Jennifer had done was lift up the glass front of the cabinet containing the stuffed magpie. Jennifer closed the case, sheepishly hung her head, and went and hid behind some of the other girls. Myself, and several others, who obviously thought Miss Loveless' reaction was somewhat disproportionate for what had occurred, looked at her as if to ask, but without actually saying it, 'was that really necessary?' and of course she (Miss Loveless) saw us all staring at her and asking the unstated question. Although beautiful, I noticed that she did look rather hollow-eyed and tired, and so assumed this had contributed to her unnecessarily harsh reaction. However, after sensing our disapproval, she did continue in a gentler tone,

"The exhibits are delicate, children. How many more times do I have to tell you? Please don't touch. If I see anyone else touching the cases, there will be no film show, and we will go back to the classroom, and you will spend the rest of this afternoon reading your text-books. Does everyone understand?"

There was a mumbled, "Yes, Miss."

This obviously wasn't considered good enough, as she then added a little more sternly,

"Well?"

"Yes, Miss," we all mumbled again, only a bit louder this time.

Why the fuss? For the life of me, I couldn't see what was so precious about the fusty exhibits that warranted such a dire threat such as cancelling a slide show?

"Good. Now. David, can you put the slide projector on the stand in front of the other one? And you girls," she said to the small gaggle that had gathered around Jennifer, "will you close the blinds, please?"

She then walked over to Jennifer and put her arm round her, "I'm sorry if I was cross with you just now, Jennifer. But please don't touch. Are you all right now? Are you sure?"

Jennifer looked up at her and smiled weakly.

"Good," said Miss Lovelies and pulled Jennifer to her and gave her a hug.

"I wish she'd hug me like that!" said Teddy under his breath, having seen Jennifer's head pressed against Miss Lovelies' 'lovelies'.

"You know what you've got to do then," said his brother with a grin, "but not right now, wait until the end of the lesson; we want to see the slide show first. Then, if you're lucky, she'll keep you in detention and hug you for half an hour," he added with a snigger.

However, before all of this and just before poor Jennifer had been told off, I'd noticed that our resident goth, Marianne Cole, had lifted up the bell-jar which contained the bat. Needless to say, when Miss Loveless started scolding Jennifer, Marianne quickly and quietly replaced the glass bell. She looked across at me and realising that I'd seen her replacing the bell-jar, put a single finger up to and across her lips. I'd winked back, and she'd smiled, and for the first time I'd noticed that she was pretty when she smiled. We'd held each other's eyes for a second or two before we'd both looked away and started showing our silent disapproval of Miss Loveless' verbal assault on poor Jennifer.

As the girls started pulling down the blinds, we boys started to set out the chairs, and this gave the Thompsons and I a chance to have a look at the fox. I walked over to the cabinet, to Renard, and looked at him. Yes, he was still in his box, but, was there something different about him? Was he in precisely the same position? I felt certain that there was something that I was just not seeing. You know, something hidden in plain sight.

"Don't just stand there. Come and have a look," I whispered between clenched teeth to the two Thompsons.

Somewhat warily, they came across to the cabinet.

"You see," I said to Teddy, "Renard is still there."

But what I was really hoping was that they would also feel, as I did, that there was something different about him, and I was hoping that they would be able to identify it.

"Yeah, I know Tom, but honestly it weren't there on Saturday night," said Teddy under his breath.

"Hey! Look at its snout," said Bobby, "has it got more hair than I remember?" Was this Bobby's way of saying 'it *has* got more hair'? Yes! I was as sure as I could be that the snout had been all-but worn down to the leather of the skin, but there it was now, right in front of us, and not looking as poorly as I'd remembered. Indeed, this rather too hurried inspection did suggest that dear old Renard looked in remarkably good health for a dead fox that had last paid a visit to a taxidermist something like a hundred years ago.

"Thomas, Edward, Robert, will you sit down please. We are ready to start now," said Miss Loveless.

Someone turned out the light and a picture of a glacier appeared on the screen. Miss Loveless then started to talk about glaciation and erosion, moraine, drumlins, arêtes, pyramidal peaks, U-shaped valleys and so on, with a new slide being displayed to illustrate the newly mentioned geographic feature.

"Now do you believe me?" whispered Teddy.

"It's certainly odd," I had to admit. "It would be nice to get a good look at it without having Miss Lovelies watching our every move."

"Yeah, it would."

"Edward Thompson, if you don't stop talking you can go and stand outside."

"And then you'll get a hug afterwards," whispered his brother.

The three of us nearly burst out laughing, but somehow just managed to hold things together.

Chapter 6

That Same Evening.

As I've already explained, my parents, particularly my mother, didn't approve of my friendship with the Thompson twins, so I'd had to make up some excuse for wanting to go out at 8.15pm armed with a torch. What that excuse was, I now have no idea, though I think I can safely assume that whatever it was, my parents probably didn't believe it, but they let me go anyway. Teddy, Bobby and I met at the village green at 8.30pm, as had previously been agreed, and from there, we headed off on our mission to discover the truth about the stuffed fox.

Of course we didn't go into the school via the main entrance; only rank amateurs would have done that," enthused Tom, obviously enjoying play-acting his childhood self.

"Instead, in the intermittent moonlight of that night, we walked nonchalantly right past it continuing down the road in the direction of the stone bridge over the river. Part way along the road, after checking that no one was watching us, Bobby opened a gate and we slipped quickly through and into the adjacent field. Hugging the line of the hedge, we walked stealthily back in the direction of the school. When we arrived at the wire link fence, which separated the field from the school playground, we turned left and followed the fence for a bit until Bobby suddenly stopped and pulled back a section of it.

"Here," he whispered.

We climbed through the hole and rapidly ran a few metres to the back of the museum/film room hut. Even Simon Templar would not have done this better than we did. After a quick look round, just to make doubly certain that no one was watching us or was already in the building - we international agents couldn't be too careful - we hurried up the steps, unlocked and opened the door, and went in.

Although, as I have already mentioned, I had entered the hut 'illegally' in daylight, I'd never done anything like this before. My heart was in my mouth and I was breathing rapidly. The moonshine wasn't as constant as I would have wished, and with clouds scudding across the sky, the room was pitch black one minute and bathed in pale greenish-blue moonlight the next. Under this intermittent lighting and with the odd exhibits spread out around it, the room looked amazingly spooky, as if part of a Hammer Horror film set. The pale green-blue light variously lit up the inhabitants of the cases, or flashed off the bottle-green glass which surrounded them. Can you imagine how the eagle owl or whatever-it-was, and the crow looked? You could have sworn that the owl had just blinked and that the crow, with its head down and beak open was squawking at you; Cwark! Cwark! '*We* know you are in here!' The place gave me the creeps and my nerves were ready to snap at any minute.

However, as said, we were on a mission, so there was no time for whimpish things like frayed nerves! We had come to check on the fox, the magpie and the bat. And the bat? Yes, after getting Teddy and Bobby to swear their silence, I had told them about Marianne Cole having lifted the bell-jar on the bat. So we were going to check that one, as well as on old Renard and Jennifer's magpie.

If you never done this," explained Tom with a smile, "take my word for it, that it is one thing to walk round a classroom in daylight and easily see where everything is, but a totally different thing to go round that same room in intermittent moonshine, with one's heart in one's mouth, and try to do the same.

As I recall we found the fox's display cabinet without too much difficulty; it was one of the big ones, the only one bigger being that which contained the leaping, though more accurately best described as 'the collapsing goat,' 'Capricornus'. However, inspection of the fox in intermittent moonlight, even when aided by a bit of torch light, didn't really tell us any more than we had already gleaned from our hasty inspection of earlier-on that afternoon.

Next, was the magpie. This was in a much smaller case, and there were several of those, all of about the same size and so it was not so easy to locate. And finally there was the bat, which was in a bell-jar and again, there were several of those, and they were all, near enough, exactly the same size. The moonlight was constantly being switched on and off by the passing clouds, so one minute all was bathed in blue-green light, and the next plunged into blackness when you couldn't see a thing. I remember we split up and walked slowly down the rows trying to make out what was in each case and what was in each bell-jar. After what seemed an age, Teddy suddenly whispered,

"I've found the magpie."

Bobby and I made our way over to Teddy who, when we'd joined him, turned on his torch and shone it at the bird. Well, yes, it was the magpie and it was definitely there, so no problems on that front. To be honest, it was impossible, in the available light, to see whether it had had the same luck as the fox and managed to improve its appearance in the time that had elapsed between Jennifer lifting the cabinet front and us looking at it then.

"Looks the same to me," whispered Teddy.

"And to me," I added in a similarly hushed voice.

"OK," said Teddy snapping off the torch, "Two down, one to go."

"Just a minute," said Bobby slowly, "Put some light on the base, Ted."

Teddy switched the torch back on again and shone it on to the base of the cabinet.

"Oh no!"

"Ssh!"

There, sitting on the base and inside the cabinet, was a ring. It looked like a diamond ring.

"I think we had better leave it where it is," said Teddy, almost instinctively, "We don't want to get accused of stealing that."

"But how on earth did it get there?" I ventured.

"I think we can guess that," said Bobby. "The fox has been out ...." And he left the sentence hanging in the air with an unstated, 'and we know what the fox has done.'

The room felt as if it had gone suddenly cold as it dawned on us that something very strange was going on.

"Let's find the bat and get the hell out of here," said Teddy voicing the thoughts of all three of us. The fun had suddenly gone out of the adventure, as there appeared to be something horribly unnerving, almost sinister, about what seemed to have happened, or was it, 'what was happening?'

We found the groups of bell-jars, but trying to see exactly what was in each was not easy. The clouds scudding across the moon, switching on and switching off its light, did nothing to help. All the exhibits were of about the same size, and none seemed to contain the bat.

"It's got to be somewhere."

"Bring the torch over here, Ted," said Bobby. "We'll go through each group of jars."

As soon as the torch shone on the bell-jars, we saw that it lit them up like large pieces of a chandelier, or lenses of a lighthouse, and for a horrible moment felt certain that if anyone had looked towards the school, they would have seen that we were there. Fortunately, the hut we were in was well shielded from the village proper by the adjacent hut. However the windows of both were at the same level, and so the other hut did not offer that much protection from any curious eyes that might have been looking in our direction. We quickly went through the first group of jars. Teddy switched the torch off as soon as we had confirmed that all the residents were at home.

On to the next lot. Again, no bat, and each jar had an occupant. And so to the third and final batch.

"Yes. Yes. Yes. Oh no!"

The jar, which no doubt should have contained the bat, contained nothing other than the grotty piece of branch from which it should have been hanging. The bat was, oh-so-obviously, missing.

We stood there in the dark, in a state of semi-shock, wondering what to do, until Bobby broke the silence.

"Of course it won't be there, it's a bat," he said. "The magpie is a daytime bird, so it had to come back during daylight hours and before nightfall. The bat is nocturnal, a bit like the fox. So it will be out at night, and, more than likely, will come back just before dawn."

Such was the state of our nerves that we breathed a collective sigh of relief, as if Bobby's explanation had answered *everything*. However, whereas yes, it might have gone some way to explaining why the bat had not returned to its bell-jar yet, but what it most certainly *did not* explain was why a long-dead and stuffed bat should leave a bell-jar in the first place!

"Let's get out of here," I said, not knowing if my nerves could stand a second longer of this.

And that's exactly what we did.

When out of the building and back on the road, back in a safer environment where dead things didn't disappear out of cases, I ventured,

"One of us is going to have to verify that the bat is back in its place tomorrow."

"Yeah," said Teddy, "and what about that ring?"

"Oh goodness. I'd forgotten about that."

"We can't tell anyone that we've been in the room or they'll blame us for stealing it. We'll just have to let someone else find it there."

"Yes," agreed Bobby and then he added, "If the fox has only been out once, it's more than likely the magpie will not go out again, so the ring should remain where it is until someone spots it."

Thank goodness one of us was thinking clearly. We agreed it would be best to say nothing. Strangely, now I think about it, nothing further was thought about, or indeed said about the bat.

And that was the end of that night's escapade.

When I got home and had gone up to my bedroom, I breathed a huge sigh of relief. That had been an adventure that I didn't want to repeat in a hurry. But what had happened to the bat? Where was it? And suddenly I caught myself consciously making a point of checking that the windows were shut. There was certainly something odd; no, more than odd, about what was happening. I sat down on my bed and went through what we'd discovered, and it was all too clear that that which had started out as a bit of innocent fun, suddenly wasn't so innocent, or so much fun any more.

Where had old man Syphre obtained these animals and birds? Why weren't they behaving as one would expect dead, stuffed things to behave?

I went and checked the window again before pulling the curtains.

Chapter 7

Religious Instruction.

As I have already mentioned, if Mrs Felicity Shaw did have a fault, it was that she could get a bit self-righteous and blinkered, a little too sure when discussing religion, and again, as already said, she took us for Religious Instruction. Don't forget that in those days, this was not as it is now. It was not about instruction in religions, it was about instruction in Protestant, Church of England, Christianity. Back in those days, as far as our school was concerned, other religions quite simply didn't exist, and what is more, it *was assumed* that you believed in Protestant, Church of England, Christianity as well, though that was, just, beginning to change.

Although it probably did not occur at precisely this point in my story, the one R.I. lesson of this period, which both illustrates the changing attitude and sticks in my mind, is the one when Felicity and Bobby Thompson crossed swords, though whether that is the most appropriate metaphor to use to describe the events of that lesson is another matter. I will include the events of that lesson here, and then we can get back to the story proper," explained Tom.

"It went something like this, though, as with the rest of this story, this little interlude is from my memory.

Felicity was already waiting for us in the classroom that day, as we all filed in and took our places. After the usual 'Good morning, everyone' and 'Good morning, Miss,' she asked;

"And where did we get to last time? Yes, Sheila."

"Moses had just got the Ten Commandments from God and had come down from the Mount, Miss."

"And?"

"All the people were worshipping a golden calf, Miss," answered an enthusiastic Sheila.

"That's right. And what did he do then?"

After a brief pause and no response from Sheila, Bobby Thompson put up his hand.

"Yes, Robert."

"He went and smashed the calf and made the people worship what *he* had chosen to believe in," he answered somewhat provocatively.

"Indeed, he did. And do I suppose Robert, that you think that he was wrong?" she said in a slightly haughty tone, which was enough to let Bobby know that he had scored a hit!

"Of course it was, Miss. Why couldn't the people worship a golden calf if they wanted to? It wasn't doing Moses any harm and no-one was saying that *he* had to worship the calf if he didn't want to. Why couldn't he just leave them alone to worship what they wished to, instead of insisting that he was right and that everyone else was wrong? The calf was made from *their* gold after all, not his; they'd melted down their own gold. How would he have liked it if the roles had been reversed and they had smashed up his property and insisted that he'd had to worship their calf?"

Felicity was obviously a little taken aback by Bobby's answer and responded with,

"So do I take it Robert that you see nothing wrong in worshipping a calf?"

"No Miss, as long as it does no harm to others."

"But the Ten Commandments clearly state that 'Thou shalt have no other gods before me,' and 'Thou shalt not make unto thee any graven image.'[6]" replied Felicity.

Bobby looked at her blankly as if to say, 'So what? That is not an answer.' But Bobby just couldn't resist tossing a bit of fat into the fire,

"But, the Ten Commandments, Miss, are commandments of the religion that Moses had chosen to believe in and had nothing whatsoever to do with the religion of those who had chosen to worship the calf. Why couldn't Moses believe in that which he wished to believe in and leave the others to believe in that which they wished to? Why did he have to start a fight?"

Oh dear! It was obvious that the lesson was not going in the direction that Felicity had initially envisaged. However, instead of responding to Bobby's deliberately provocative observations, she cleverly side-stepped this and said,

"I had thought that today's lesson would be about the Exodus. However, if you wish, we could have a discussion on the more general subject of religion and leave the Exodus for another day. Hands up, those who would prefer a discussion on religion."

To my surprise, an amazing number of hands went up. I say surprise, because I had no idea that so many in our class had any interest whatsoever.

"Right," said Felicity. "So can anyone tell me why we need religion?"

Her question was met by a sea of blank faces. Now you can understand why I'd thought that so many had no interest in this subject!

"Anyone?"

Bobby Thompson slowly raised his hand. Poor Felicity looked round the class to see if there was anyone else she could ask other than Bobby, and upon seeing there was not, said,

---

[6] Exodus 20:3 and 4

"Yes, Robert."

"We don't, Miss."

"You mean, don't need religion?" she queried.

"No, Miss. We don't *need* to worship anything."

"So how would we know the difference between right and wrong?"

"We don't need religion to tell us that," replied Bobby. "Ethics and morals will do that. Religion is about doctrine and dogma, not to mention, money and power."

Felicity listened and raised her eyebrows.

"Don't you think you are being just a touch harsh, Robert?"

"No Miss," said Bobby flatly.

"We all know it is wrong to kill people. Indeed, one of the Ten Commandments states, 'Thou shalt not kill' [7], yet the Crusades were carried out on the express orders of the Pope, the head of the Catholic Church, a supposedly religious man, and thousands were slaughtered in the name of that religion because they were deemed by this man to be 'Infidels', almost sub-human. Either his religion didn't inform him of the difference between right and wrong, or he completely ignored its own Commandments. And if the man in charge completely ignores any supposed teaching and tenets of the religion and church which he represents, then it is not unreasonable to conclude that the teaching and tenets which the religion purports to hold, are *not* in fact held by it. This exemplifies the same attitude as shown by Moses; namely, 'I'm right, you're wrong' and is nothing to do with ethics and morals and what is actually right and wrong."

I wouldn't like to swear that schoolboy Bobby used those actual words, but that was the general gist of what he said," Tom

---

[7] Exodus 21:13

explained, before continuing with,

"Felicity was most certainly surprised by Bobby's answer, but before she could compose herself and reply, Bobby charged on.

"If religion and the church were a true source for ethical and moral guidance, why did the Catholics and the Protestants, both supposedly religious and both supposedly believing in the same God, start fighting each other? And this was not in what some these days might claim was an uncivilised part of the world, it was right here in this country. Simple history would suggest that we would have been much better off without religion."

Poor Felicity! And don't forget she taught us history, and so was only too well aware of what Bobby was talking about. I felt for her, as I was certain that she had not anticipated this logically reasoned, verbal onslaught from Bobby. How, I wondered, was she going to respond to this? But she did, and generously conceded,

"Yes, Robert is correct, there have been some dreadful and senseless wars." And then she added, "but I am not so sure that you can condemn religion just because some foolish and evil men have fought over it. People fight over all sorts of things and we don't usually blame the fight on the thing that they are fighting over."

Bobby nodded, conceding that, yes, Felicity did have a point.

"Religion also gives a society its structure," she continued.

Bobby had his hand up again and almost before Felicity gave him the floor, he started off with,

"But hasn't religion, organised religion, been more about control and amassing wealth, power and influence to itself, rather than placing the needs of the people first?"

"Possibly," said Felicity surprisingly; well I thought so, given that I wasn't expecting her to agree with Bobby. "But are not control, wealth and power what men desire, and not what the religion itself requires?"

I saw Bobby nodding again before responding with,

"But Miss, surely that is not quite the case."

"Oh?"

"Because doesn't the Christian religion in fact encourage these traits? The parable of The Talents all-but states that the making of money, or the amassing of wealth, is good."

"One mustn't take that parable too literally, Robert," replied Felicity, "The word 'talent' can also be interpreted as ability, or initiative. Hence, the person who makes use of his abilities should be rewarded."

"Yes Miss, we can interpret it that way, but it is very clear in the parable that a Talent is a coin, and hence that the parable is about making money. When the lord rebukes the servant who still has the one Talent he says, 'thou oughtest therefore to have put my money to the exchangers, and then at my coming I should have received mine own with usury.'[8] This is not a metaphor, Miss, this is all about making profit and amassing wealth and the parable is holding this up as a good thing. And as for control and power, in Exodus we are told ....," continued Bobby, quickly leafing through his Bible, ".... that 'for I the Lord thy God am a jealous God, visiting the iniquity of the fathers upon the children unto the third and fourth generation of them that hate me.'[9] Surely Miss, this is one hundred percent about control and power. There is not a hint of tolerance, or freedom of choice in it. And what about ....," and there was another brief pause as again, Bobby amazingly quickly and accurately located his next quotation, 'I will make mine arrows drunk with blood, and my sword shall devour flesh; and that with the blood of the slain and of the captives, from the

---

8 Matthew 25:27
9 Exodus 20:5

beginning of revenges upon the enemy,' in Deuteronomy?[10] Or in Nahum, where it is stated, 'God is jealous, and the Lord revengeth; the Lord revengeth, and is furious; the Lord will take vengeance on his adversaries, and he reserveth wrath for his enemies.'?[11] I am sorry Miss, but it is not true that the evil in the world is just down to men. Here in this very book, vengeance, revenge, war and killing are esteemed and God is quoted as being jealous, taking revenge and vengeance, and visiting iniquity and wrath, not only on those who He sees as having slighted Him, but also on their entirely innocent children; 'unto the third and fourth generation!' It is not just men who are evil, Miss, it is actually written into the religion."

As I said at the start of this section, R.I. in those days was about instruction in Protestant, Church of England, Christianity, and not about instruction in religions in general. These days, we know that the three monotheistic religions all share the same roots, and yes, all share the same lack of tolerance, and threats of wrath and revenge. Felicity was probably not prepared for any of this and, it has to be said, your average school boy is not usually as sharp as a Bobby Thompson.

"Yes," said Felicity slowly, while obviously trying to collect her thoughts and form a reasoned response to Bobby. "You are right Robert, the Bible does contain some, what we might regard these days as, unpalatable assertions."

Then, turning to the rest of us, she continued,

"However, what Robert has quoted is from the Old Testament and this is very much a collection of ancient books which gives voice to men's views before the birth of Jesus Christ, and, as I am sure you will concede, Robert, his message was not about revenge, vengeance and visiting iniquity and wrath on anyone."

---

[10] Deuteronomy 32:42
[11] Nahum 1:2

"Um, Miss," said Teddy, raising his hand to come to the aid of his brother.

"Yes Edward."

"The Parable of the Talents, about the making of money, is in the New Testament, Miss."

"Yes it is Edward."

But this didn't stop Teddy, who just pushed on, rather like his brother,

"Hebrews 10:30 says, 'For we know him that hath said, Vengeance belongeth unto me, I will recompense, saith the Lord. And again, The Lord shall judge his people.' And in Paul's Second Epistle to the Thessalonians he states, 'When the Lord Jesus shall be revealed from heaven with his mighty angels, in flaming fire taking vengeance on them that know not God, and that obey not the gospel of our Lord Jesus toward all men.'[12] Intolerance, power and the threat of violence is not just in the Old Testament, Miss."

Poor Felicity was on the back foot again and realised it.

"Yes," she said slowly, "but doesn't Paul then go on to say, 'See that none render evil for evil unto any man; but ever follow that which is good[13]?'

However, there was no sense of triumph in her voice as she must have realised that this quotation did not undo the earlier ones that Teddy had cited.

"We must remember that the Bible was written hundreds of years ago. Elements of it which may seem strange to us these days are only so because the ways of expressing ourselves have changed over time and perhaps successive translations have not taken this into account?" Felicity explained, somewhat lamely

---

[12] Thessalonians 1:8
[13] Thessalonians 5:15

I thought, as I couldn't see how any of those quotations could have been interpreted in anyway differently, which was what she seemed to be suggesting.

No one said anything. I don't think I'd ever known our class to be so quiet.

Then Felicity broke the spell, and unusually for those days, actually asked,

"Hands up, those who believe in God."

A few of the girls' hands went up, which no doubt pleased her as she visibly brightened at the sight of this.

"So, who can tell me why they believe? Yes, Sheila."

"I believe in God, Miss, because I know He will keep me away from evil and safe from harm."

Bobby groaned and slumped down in his desk.

"I heard that Robert Thompson! There is no need to be rude," said a suddenly stern Mrs Shaw.

"Sorry, Miss," apologised Bobby, but almost immediately asked, "but haven't you just changed the subject of our discussion from religion to belief?"

"Yes, if you wish to be pedantic about it," she said, the sternness now gone from her voice, "but the two are very closely linked. We, humans, need to believe. We need to believe .... for example, that the sun is going to rise every morning."

Bobby's hand was already up.

"Yes, Robert," said Felicity with just the slightest hint of resigned annoyance in her voice.

"That is knowledge, Miss, not belief. Belief may be required in a society where people do not understand that our Earth is spinning on its axis and revolving around the sun, but when that is known ...." he said with a shrug as if to suggest that there was no more to say on the subject, as it was after all, blindingly obvious! Well, to Bobby it was, even if some of the rest of us still had some difficulty understanding how this resulted in the changing seasons and all-day winter darkness and summer midnight sun in arctic regions.

"No, I grant you that was not a good example," said Felicity, who obviously realised that she had plucked her example out of the air rather too quickly, and certainly too quickly if she had Bobby Thompson in her class.

"Let me give you another one," she offered. "What about the belief that you all have parents who love you? You cannot prove this in factual or scientific terms. Yes, of course you can say, 'I know my parents love me because they gave me this or that for my birthday,' but if you think about it that doesn't actually prove anything, other than perhaps how much money your parents have to spend. Love is not measurable and therefore not provable. We can't see, taste or touch it, but we know when it is there and when it is not. Is that knowledge? Or is it belief? Or is it a bit of both?"

I noticed that Bobby didn't challenge her on this and for the second time that morning there was again complete silence as we all pondered on something that we had never considered thinking about before.

"I noticed that not many of you boys put up your hands just now," said Felicity. "How can you all be so sure that God does not exist?"

Teddy Thompson raised his hand again, though a little more hesitantly this time. Felicity continued to look around the class. Whereas she might have been partially relieved that she didn't have to ask Bobby yet again, she obviously thought that the discussion ought to be opened up to include the rest of the class and not just the Thompsons. However, left with no choice, she asked,

"Yes, Edward."

"But Miss, how can you be so sure that He does?"

"Because I am Edward. I believe there is love and goodness in this world. Don't you believe in these?"

"Oh yes Miss, but there is also hatred and evil in the world."

"Yes, there certainly are."

Bobby had his hand up again, and I could see that the usually so-patient Felicity had a little of an 'oh no, not again!' expression on her face, but her nature was such that she could not ignore Bobby even though she must have found it a touch exasperating having to argue with him.

"So *if* evil exists, Miss, how does that prove that God exists?" commenced Bobby.

He let this question hang for a second before continuing,

"We all know that there is right and wrong, and that good and evil exist, but neither depends upon the existence or otherwise of a god. They are just different ways of describing good and bad experiences in our lives. They do not prove the existence of a god, or the truth of a god."

"No, they don't," acknowledged Felicity. "But religion is not about proof, it is about belief and faith, belief that goodness and love can prevail, and that the world can be a better place. We need to believe that this is possible, that we can make it so, and this is where religion, which we might regard as a formalisation of our belief, comes in to it, because knowing our frailties as men and women we need to believe that there is something larger and better than ourselves; a god, who will give us the strength to do this. And we need to have faith in that god, faith in God, faith that He loves us, will look after us, keep us from harm and guide us. 'Faith is the substance of things hoped for, the evidence of things not seen'[14].

And so yes, I do believe in a God that sent His only son to die for us, to atone for our sins, and I know that because He has made that ultimate sacrifice for us, that He does love us and will look after us, will keep us safe, will keep us away from and protect us against evil, will lift us up when we lose our enthusiasm and are tired, and will be there to carry us through when the odds seem stacked against us, even in our darkest moments when there appears to be no hope. We need God to guide us, and we need religion to structure our belief."

Blimey! What can I say? Even cynical Bobby had sat up straight and was looking at her. And more telling was his expression, which was no longer that of a smug knowing of the rightness of his argument, but one of realising that perhaps Felicity was also right, albeit that she was talking about something completely different, something that had nothing to do with logic, hard facts and provable truths, but nonetheless was just as valid.

Felicity concluded with a quiet, "That is all for today," and we started to collect our things and file out.

And as I did so, I noticed that Bobby had gone over to Felicity and that the pair of them were talking. Bobby had obviously appreciated something in what Felicity had just said, and as I have mentioned before, Felicity didn't hold a grudge, even against her most argumentative pupils.

---

[14] Hebrews 11:1

Chapter 8

The Exorcism.

During the course of the week that followed our nocturnal visit to the film-room hut, the ring was discovered by one of the kids in one of the other classes and, as Tommy had predicted, Old Badger wanted to know who had put it there. The same class also observed that the bat was missing, though as we knew, was not just missing, but *still* missing. This was odd, as we had expected it to return to the bell-jar.

The owner of the ring was surprisingly quickly discovered; it was Felicity. As I have already mentioned, she had only recently got married, and as her ring was still relatively new and she hadn't wanted to get it dirty, she had, we learned later, apparently taken it off and put it on the garden table while she'd dug up some vegetables in her garden. When she turned round, the ring was gone. Of course neither she, nor her husband Aidan, had any idea where it had gone, and both were over-joyed when it was found just a few days later. However, although we didn't know this at the time, obviously both they and everyone else, were mystified as to how it had ended up being found in the school, and in a cabinet containing a stuffed magpie.

Old Badger, so predictably, immediately jumped to the conclusion that one of the pupils, by which he meant one of the boys, had stolen it and placed it in the cabinet possibly as some sort of a prank and, perhaps needless to say, the Thompson twins were, as Teddy had feared would be the case, the most likely suspects. However, Old Badger had no proof whatsoever, and fortunately for the twins, Felicity had obviously come to their defence as she knew exactly where she had left her ring and that neither of the Thompsons had been in her garden while she was digging up her vegetables.

The next day, when Old Badger stood up in assembly, we all feared the worst and so were completely taken by surprise when, instead of talking about Felicity's ring, he said,

"There have been reports of some strange happenings vis-a-vis the zoological specimens that are currently housed in the film room. I can assure you all that there is no truth whatsoever in any of the rumours that have been circulating and that there are perfectly logical explanations for everything that is claimed to have happened. However, in order just to put everyone's mind at rest, I have spoken with our Vicar, the Reverend Bitterling, and he has kindly offered to come and say a prayer and carry out an exorcism in the room on Thursday, 31 October."

Exorcism?! What was all this about?

Of course, Old Badger didn't elaborate on 'the rumours that were not supposed to be true', and neither did he give us any hint as to the 'perfectly logical explanations' either. And more tellingly still, neither did he explain why, if the rumours were all untrue and there were such perfectly logical explanations for everything, our vicar, the Reverend Bitterling, had been asked, and was prepared to take time to come into the school to say a bit of mumbo-jumbo? Even we realised that 'the truth', whatever it was, was not certain, was not undeniable. Indeed, it was very much looking as if it had yet to be decided upon. Something was up, and something was worrying not just us, but obviously some of the adults as well. Had they discussed the odd disappearance and then even stranger reappearance of Felicity's ring? She obviously knew where and when she had taken it off, and so knew with absolute certainty that it had not been stolen by any of us boys. So, were our teachers also asking themselves how Felicity's ring had got from her garden table to the base of the case containing the stuffed magpie? Were the adults just as mystified as we were, and was this exorcism their answer to sorting this mystery out, or at the very least their attempt at putting a lid on it? And then, the final oddity in all of this was that this exorcism was going to be carried out on one of the most pagan days of the year, namely, Halloween, which certainly was a strange choice of date to be carrying out a Christian ceremony. However, as the day following Halloween was All Saints Day and no doubt the Reverend Bitterling would be busy then, perhaps he wasn't taking this as seriously as Old Badger appeared to be suggesting and was just squeezing it in before-hand?

We were part-way through our maths class on the Thursday morning when Old Badger and the Reverend Bitterling came into the classroom. Badger had a few words with Miss Loveless, who then announced to us that we would all be attending the exorcism ceremony in the film room. Why our class had been chosen to attend this, I don't know. I suppose Old Badger was assuming that because we had been the class most closely involved with these 'specimens' - we'd unpacked them and placed them in the film projection room after all - and so hence that it was ourselves that needed to witness this 'purging of evil' from them; though this did rather presuppose that they were in need of this 'purging'. It was also possible of course, that he'd assumed that it had probably been our class that had started most of his so-called 'untrue rumours' and hence that it was this that possibly suggested that our presence was required? And finally, we could be absolutely certain that he could not let go of the fact that the Thompson twins were, in spite of all evidence to the contrary, still his prime suspects. So our class's attendance, as representatives of the pupils of the school, would witness that the 'strange incidents,' all of which we had been assured were untrue, had been 'properly dealt with.'

And it is interesting to note," said Tom, as an aside, "that these days some rumour about some politician is always apparently untrue, and of course the Prime Minister still has full confidence in that individual, but, in spite of the fact that whatever-it-is, is so patently untrue, just to put everyone's mind at rest, he or she will ask the Ethics and Standards Committee to look into the business and give their ruling and then …. just few days later, suddenly the Prime Minister no longer has full confidence in the now disgraced miscreant and they are summarily sacked from whichever position they were previously holding! Truth in politics most certainly has nothing to do with that which is true or not true, and everything to do with that which can or can't be legally proven, irrespective of whether or not it is actually true.

So, back in my story.

Old Badger, in his full formal dress of black cloak and mortar board, together with the Reverend Bitterling, also in his full formal dress of black cassock and cloak with ecclesiastic purple lining and gold embroidered trims, led us out of our school classroom, down its set of steps to the playground, across the playground, then up another set of steps and into the film room. Once there, we were placed at the screen end of the room. Miss Lovelies, in a blouse which was buttoned up tight to her neck that morning, stood with us, while Old Badger and the Reverend Bitterling went to the other end of the room where a single desk had already been set out in front of the projector. Old Badger stood off to one side, facing us. The Reverend Bitterling placed his bag on the floor behind the desk and from it produced a white and purple cloth which he spread out over the desk. On this, he placed a small wooden crucifix in a stand. Then he set down two cream coloured church candles, each in a silver candlestick, one on each side of it. He lit the candles. After this, he produced a Bible and placed it unopened, on the desk. Finally, he took out a small black leather-bound book, which he opened and glanced at, before putting it down on the desk. We were then required to say the Lord's Prayer. After the amen, Bitterling - though perhaps I should refer to him as the Reverend Bitterling? - picked up the crucifix from its stand and placed it in the fist of his left hand. He then crossed himself with his free hand and after placing it on the Bible, held his fist at the first group of display cases and bell-jars, cleared his throat and in a firm voice said,

"In the name of the Father, the Son and the Holy Ghost, I command that any and all evil spirits in, around or attached to these zoological specimens depart hence forth and never to return."

Looking round the faces of our class, I could see some, like Sheila Simonds, with mouth open and eyes wide, looked almost terrified, while others, like the Thompson twins, thought the whole thing a complete joke and appeared to be having difficulty holding back their laughter. However, even Teddy and Bobby Thompson gave the ceremony their full attention when, after the Reverend Bitterling had read out the same exorcising incantation to a group of cases and jars, there was a loud crack and one of the jars suddenly shattered, spraying glass in all directions over the desk and floor. After that, you could have heard a pin drop. The Reverend Bitterling went deathly white, and for a moment appeared at a complete loss for words. Old Badger, the true soldier, didn't move, but I guessed probably got a few more white hairs as a result of this, and we all clearly heard Marianne Cole whisper,

"That was the jar that had contained the bat."

The Reverend Bitterling tried to pull himself together and continue as if nothing unusual had happened, though his pretence at this was given away by his rather too hurriedly turning his attention to the next group of exhibits. So there was no mistaking whatsoever that he had been frightened. No, not just shocked like most of us present who really had no idea of what all this exorcising was about, but frightened, really frightened, and this, I assumed, was because he *did know* what all this was about.

As I was staring at the broken glass on the desk and floor, Marianne's words replayed in my head, 'That was the jar that had contained the bat', and I realised that the breaking of the jar meant that the bat could now no longer return, because it had nowhere to return to. So was it, as a result of this event, destined, like some doomed accursed spirit, like some nocturnal Flying Dutchman, to fly the night sky forever? And what did that mean for us?

The Reverend Bitterling finished his incantations, packed away the items that he had brought with him, and with somewhat unbecoming haste - or was it fearful haste? - left the room without saying anything further, with Old Badger in his wake. Our class and Miss Loveless, were simply left standing there. Was the little ceremony that was supposed to show that both the 'strange incidents' for which there were 'perfectly logical explanations' and the rumours which had 'had no truth in them' had been 'properly dealt with,' now over? If so, unfortunately, it had achieved none of its objectives. Indeed, it had only resulted in yet another 'strange incident' for which there appeared to be no 'perfectly logical explanation,' which, in turn, could only reinforce the rumours which had 'had no truth in them.'

As it became apparent that the ceremony was over, Miss Loveless indicated that we should all go back to our classroom. When back there, I noticed, and I was certain that Teddy Thompson had also noticed, that the top two buttons of Miss Louise's blouse had become undone again; a sign perhaps, that all was back to normal?

Chapter 9

Halloween.

It goes without saying that what we had all been waiting for was the evening of Halloween; the last day in October, the eve of All Saints' Day, or All Hallows' Day, on the 1st November. Of course we had no interest whatsoever in the saints, or their days. What we wanted was ghosts, ghouls, skeletons, witches and so on, and as you can probably guess, this was Marianne Cole's evening of the year. Quite unexpectedly, I found myself wondering what she would be dressed as? And just as unexpectedly, I was surprised to observe in myself that prior to my noticing her lifting up the bell-jar on the bat that day, I hadn't really noticed her, and yet, now, there I was thinking about her and also wondering whether I would meet up with her at some point in the evening .... and yes, I found myself noting, she was pretty when she smiled .... and it would be nice if ....

Now, I need to tell you about Halloween, as it was in those days," said Tom, in a more serious voice.

"On the actual evening, we all used to dress up in some costume, which, with the help of our mothers, we had been making over the previous few weeks. Witches were, of course, popular amongst the girls, and some put an amazing amount of effort into their costumes, which really were surprisingly elaborate, complete with with spider's webs and so on. At the other end of the spectrum was the 'bed sheet over the head' style of ghost, which were popular amongst the boys because they didn't require too much, or indeed, any imagination or effort to produce. Back in those days, you couldn't go out and buy a mask or costume because, quite simply, they didn't exist, there were none to buy. So there were no zombies wandering around with axes in their heads, or anything of that type. However that said, a number of us were a little more inventive and made up masks for the evening. That year, as I recall, I had made a rather good - well, I thought it was - papier-mâché ghoul's head mask, which was held on by an elastic band.

Ever since the clocks had gone back, I had been making this thing. Firstly," Tom explained for the benefit of the younger members in the group, "I'd formed a plasticine mould for this masterpiece and then covered that with layers of little pieces of flour-paste soaked paper. After it had dried out, I'd gouged out the plasticine and finally painted the resulting mask. However, as I remember, my real pride and joy that year was my jack-o'-lantern. Somehow I'd managed to get hold of a nicely deformed turnip which was round at the top and then had a bit of a waist to it so that it looked rather like an upside-down large pear. I'd hollowed this out and then sculpted a passing resemblance of a skull into it. I remember feeling quite chuffed at the end result and rather hoped that I might win a prize for it. Of course, it never occurred to me that my ghoul's head mask and the skull sculpted turnip were just a bit similar. But maybe that was the idea. I can't remember.

So, armed with our orange glowing candle-lit turnips and dressed to kill - so sorry, I just couldn't resist that pun! - we walked about in groups around the village playing pranks on those unwise enough to have chosen to live in the heart of the village. There, we haunted houses by tapping on windows or knocking on doors before running away and hiding so that the occupant opened the door to find that no one was there. Of course they knew what we were up to and usually called out to say that we might have a sweet or two if we would ensure that the ghost did not return that evening.

After we'd had enough of haunting houses and were sick of eating sweets - pineapple chunks, liquorice and gobstoppers were, as I remember, the usual fare - we made our way to the village hall, where we joined the adults for barbecued sausages, baked potatoes and such like, and enjoyed various organised games such as snap apple and duck apple."

Here, Tom paused.

"Gosh," he mused, casting a glance in the direction of Verity and Bill, "Doesn't all of this sound so terribly in the past, so almost Dickensian, as if it happened centuries ago? Was it really in our life-time? It's strange how time does not seem to move forward in a steady progression, but appears to move forward in blocks, with each successive block being surprisingly different to the one preceding it. So that when you do look back, you really *do* wonder if it was you who had lived in that earlier block of time, or whether it was someone else, or perhaps whether it was some sort of a bizarre dream, which you realise that you must have inhabited, but can't quite believe that you did."

He then turned and asked young Derek and Simon,

"Are these types of games, snap apple and duck apple, still played these days?" The blank look on their faces appeared to confirm his suspicion, that they probably weren't.

"No matter, I shall explain. The aim of the game called snap apple was to try and bite an apple suspended on a long string, but without using your hands to hold it still, and that for duck apple or apple bobbing, was much the same, but instead of having the apples hung on strings, they were floating in a large, round bowl or bucket of water. Both sound fairly simple until you start trying to do it, and especially so with the likes of Teddy Thompson doing their best to put you off, or shoving your head under water.

However, I have since wondered," continued Tom, in a more pensive tone, "if although appearing to be innocent games, perhaps they were not quite so innocent after all, and were perhaps more analogous to life than we might have realised? In the playing of these games were we not metaphorically attempting to grasp knowledge; the apple being the symbol of this? And is not the obtaining of knowledge, no, not the learning of facts and figures as we all do in school, but the obtaining of knowledge, the truth of what life is about, something which always appears to elude us? 'Ever learning, and never able to come to the knowledge of the truth'[15]? At times we think that we might just grasp its meaning, feel as if we are just within reach of it, so tantalisingly close and so might just sink our metaphorical teeth into it. Yet, just like the apple hanging on the string or floating in the pail of water, that truth moves away from us and is frustratingly hard and almost impossible to grasp, always appearing to be just out of reach."

Tom paused from this reflective moment, before continuing in a breezier tone.

"The evening was all great fun, and so fortunately everyone forgot about the bat, even though there has always been a strong association of bats with Halloween. Yes, I did see Marianne Cole, dressed as a rather fetching witch, complete with a black pointed hat, just before Teddy Thompson pushed my head into the apple bucket. Our eyes had met briefly, and we'd held each other's gaze again. She'd smiled and I, with my attention on her, hadn't been as aware of what Teddy was up to as I should have been, with the result that I took a breath just as he pushed my head under. I came up coughing and spluttering and feeling as if I had swallowed half the bucket full of water, much to the amusement of Teddy and, I suppose, of Marianne. However, when I'd finished coughing and had regained my breath, I noticed that she'd gone.

---

[15] II Timothy 3: 7 & 8

Chapter 10

All Saints Day.

But, oh my goodness, talk about a calm before the storm. The news, which went round the village like wildfire the next morning, was that the Reverend Bitterling had been found dead in the church!

Apparently he was dressed in the same attire that he'd worn when he'd visited our school to carry out the exorcism. So whatever had happened, had either happened the previous afternoon or during that same evening, because one of the church wardens found him face down, prostrate in front of the altar and stone-dead on that morning of All Saints' Day. There were rumours flying about concerning some message, written in blood - of course! - on the altar cloth, which hinted at Black Magic and Devil worship, though whether there was any truth in this, I have no idea. However, what was certain, and did nothing to calm the wildest of speculation, were the gashes on the Reverend Bitterling's face. Several people saw these, so there was no doubt that they existed. Suddenly, Old Badger's claim that 'there is no truth in any of the rumours' and that 'there were perfectly logical explanations for everything that is claimed to have happened,' sounded horribly thin. What was the 'perfectly logical explanation' for this? Some dead chickens in a run and a diamond ring turning up in a zoological display case were nothing compared to it. Even one of the exhibits going missing and a shattering bell-jar were naught by comparison. Now a man was dead, and he a priest, and dead in his own church right in front of the altar! This wasn't just a bit spooky, this was downright frightening. Even the Thompson twins were a little bit subdued .... but not for long.

"Blimey," said an all-but irrepressible Teddy. "Old Bitterling, dead! Did you hear that he'd been killed as part of a Satanic ritual?"

"No?" I replied blankly, hoping he would elaborate. And he did.

"Oh yes! Apparently there was something written in blood on the altar cloth."

"Did you see it?" I asked.

"In Nomine Dei Nostri Satanus, Luciferi Excelsi,"[16] said Teddy theatrically, while crossing himself, but I noticed that he didn't actually answer my question.

"And Old Bitterling had had his cheeks slashed," he continued enthusiastically, "A slash down each side of his face Tom, which were not cuts, but looked as if the flesh had been torn open by something pointed such as a small hook or claw."

Teddy knew how to say something without actually saying it and knew that his 'a small hook or claw', would lead me to conclude 'bat'.

"Are you sure? You know who you're sounding like," I said, thinking of Marianne's ghoulish interest in small, black nocturnal mammals, and then felt myself colouring a bit at the thought of her, and, anxious that Teddy might notice, stumbled on, "and I suppose the next thing you'll be suggesting is that the bat is still at large, and reminding us that it was the Reverend Bitterling that broke the bat's bell-jar."

"Well, it was, wasn't it," said Teddy matter-of-factly.

"What was?" I said having lost the drift of the conversation, my thoughts having strayed to and then being too mixed up with those of a smiling Marianne in her witches' outfit of the previous evening.

---

[16] 'In the name of God Our Satan, the High Lucifer,' from the Satanic Mass.

"The vicar who broke the bat's bell-jar. Are you all right Tom?"

It didn't take long for everyone to know that the Reverend Bitterling had received gashes to his face, or to recall that the bat, which had gone missing from it's bell-jar, which had subsequently mysteriously shattered during Bitterling's exorcism, was still at large. Was it just coincidence that these events had happened within a day of each other, or were they connected, and were there forces at work, dark forces of which we knew nothing, and as a result of attempting to challenge them the Reverend Bitterling, our vicar, was now dead? And if the bat was still at large, what did that portend for the rest of us?

That evening, I again checked that my bedroom window was properly shut. I then stood for a while looking out into the darkness and watched a thin veil of mist ooze out of the dark, damp ground, slowly spread across the fields, thickening as it did so, and then, enveloping everything in its path, gradually creep up the valley until it smothered it. All lay still, damp, dark and silent; dead and noiseless as a graveyard on a misty autumn night.

Chapter 11

An Attempt At Biting The Apple.

Our vicar dying in that untimely manner really unnerved many in the village, and there was no doubting that either this was linked to his exorcism of those odd stuffed zoological specimens in the school's film-room, or it was an amazingly strange coincidence. I returned to wondering what old Syphre had been doing with, or indeed, using these stuffed animals for. I was also fairly certain that I had heard of, or had read about him somewhere; his name was vaguely familiar for something other than my having visited his estate with my dad. So on the Saturday, I went down to the town and popped into the newspaper offices. There, I asked the girl at the desk about Dr Maximillan Syphre, and she very helpfully went through the back issues and pulled out some illuminating articles on the man.

Apparently he had been an explorer of sorts and an amateur scientist in his lifetime and had amassed quite a collection of what were termed objet d'art. Most of this collection had gone to various museums upon his death. It was interesting to see that there was also a little article in a recent edition of the paper on the donation that he had made posthumously to our school. However, it was the older material that I was wanting to see. At last, I came across a picture of him; a rather severe-looking Victorian or Edwardian gent in stiff-looking collars and a tweedy three piece suit, taken with some strange masks and shrunken heads. And then I came across what I had been looking for, a really good spread on the man, and a sentence which made the hairs on my neck rise; apparently, he'd had a great interest in the occult.

Although this article contained exactly the same picture of

him, the reproduction in the first article I'd looked at was larger, so I returned to that one and noticed that as well as the shrunken heads, there were, in the background, several glass-fronted cases and bell-jars containing stuffed animals and birds. These were a bit behind him and so a touch out of focus, and as a result, I couldn't make out the actual animals or birds. However, it was possible to make out the broad forms of the two largest, the leaping goat and the fox. They were unmistakable, and so I guessed it was reasonable to assume that those very same cases were now sitting in our school. And if those two were, it was a fairly safe bet that all the others in that picture were also now at our school.

As I hope you'll appreciate, I knew absolutely nothing about anything so-called 'occult.' Indeed, I knew very little about what might be described as normal main-stream religion either, other than what Felicity had told us in class. Oh, I suppose like everyone, I had wild outlandish ideas, but I knew no hard facts, and so I went back to the second article where, alongside the main piece on Dr Syphre, there were separate sidebars on the subjects of Black Magic, Satanism and so on.

The first of these was about Black magic and, as I was to also discover, White magic. White magic, it seemed, was magic which did you good, whereas black magic was magic which did you harm. Sounds simple until, as the writer pointed out, in herbal medicine the same plant could both cure and kill you. So one can easily imagine that practitioners of Middle Ages' magic began to be branded White or Black depending upon their success rate."

After our group's laughter at this observation of Tom's had subsided, he continued to explain,

"Then, in addition to this, given that most of the Church's monasteries contained herb gardens, or as they were then called, 'physic gardens', it is not impossible to imagine that a bit of attempting to corner the market and blacken the opposition's name might have also come into play. Something along the lines of, 'if it came from the Church it was good, and no doubt White, whereas if it came from elsewhere it was Black, so caveat emptor[17].' No doubt there was also an unwritten clause along the lines of, 'and if we catch the blighter we'll burn him, though more usually it was a her, at the stake'; a bit like the state does metaphorically these days with those who set up stills in their garage or basement, and so deprive the exchequer of the duty that it feels it has a right to charge on spirits.

The writer went on to say that the then new Christian religion very cleverly offered the ruling group of the day divine justification for their being in and remaining in power, and in so doing, secured its own position and acceptance in the kingdoms of the day. However, the new religion didn't, and of course, couldn't offer the man in the street anything better than the old religion had, the one which it was usurping, just something a bit different, just vague promises about future salvation, redemption, heaven and so on, but nothing tangible in this life, on this earth. How could it; real-life miracles, those which actually improve the ordinary person's standard of living, are not easy to perform? So it was highly likely that those promoting the new religion derided the old, gave it the label of Black Magic, branded its gods as 'devils' and so on, in order to bolster their new religion's image.

Although the king paid handsomely for the new religion asserting his divine right to rule - in the form of lands, buildings and the ceding of tithes, etc., - a lot of the Church's wealth was extracted from the man in the street, and if he dared to disagree, it either burnt him at the stake, chopped his head off, or even waged a crusade against him; all with the king's blessing because he was only too happy to have the Church state for him that his sitting on the throne was the will of God! And all of this came from a religion that had the audacity to suggest that it was

---

[17] Let the buyer beware.

all about love, equality in the eyes of God, tolerance and understanding. I got the feeling that the writer must have known Bobby Thompson, as he or she sounded just as cynical.

Satanism didn't appear to be anything like as diabolical as I'd expected. Like Black magic, I couldn't help but wonder if Satanism hadn't also been negatively branded by the Church, simply because it opposed their line of thinking; especially as it was claimed that it possibly predated Christianity, being related to the previous pagan religions, which obviously the Christian Church was trying to usurp and eradicate. It appeared to strongly advocate learning, knowledge, inquiry, and free thought, quite the opposite of the Christian Church, which although it might have advocated learning and knowledge, most certainly had not advocated inquiry or free thought. Indeed, throughout the centuries the Christian Church appears to have condemned those who have dared to suggest anything other than accepted Church doctrine. The world is flat, is at the centre of the universe, was created in seven days and mankind in the form of Adam and Eve were made by God and set down in the Garden of Eden. Facts! The Truth! One couldn't help but feel that St Thomas Aquinas, a 13th century philosopher, who is quoted as having said, 'Clearly the person who accepts the Church as an infallible guide will believe whatever the Church teaches,' was rather sticking his neck out; though perhaps the irony in his quotation was lost? There was no doubt that the Church had tried to corner 'knowledge' for its own ends and stop the man in the street from 'eating too much of the fruits of the Tree', because it had only been when those who dared to oppose the Church's teaching had marshalled so much incontrovertible evidence that their claims could no longer be refuted, that the Church had then deigned to accept the new knowledge and sought to deny their previous false teaching by saying that what had been said in the past was always meant to be just an allegory, just a story. Yes, yes, of course it had been!

This sidebar article went on to explain that so-called demons might have been the old gods that the Christian Church was trying to obliterate and write into history. Old pagan temple sites had certainly had new Christian churches built on them. Indeed, the temples themselves had been demolished, and the very stones that they had been built with - yes, those that had been used to build a house for the devil! - had been reused to build the new churches, without it seemed, any theological qualms about the provenance of the materials used. And there was no doubt whatsoever that the old pagan ceremonies had also been usurped and rebranded with Christian versions of the same; e.g. Harvest Festival, which had been traditionally held on the date of the full moon of the autumn equinox, was moved to the nearest Sunday. Christmas replaced the older Yule or Yuletide celebrations, which had been previously held at the time of the winter solstice. The one exception appeared to be with the rebranding of Easter. This was the old pagan time of rebirth, held at the spring equinox; and apparently the name Easter, was not of Christian origin at all, but had been derived from a pagan fertility goddess, Ēostre, and furthermore, the pagan practice of the giving of eggs - a pagan symbol of birth - at this time of year, had also been retained and adopted by the new religion.

The days of the week, all derived from celestial bodies or pagan gods, were so well established that they could not be rebranded. However, Sunday, the Day of the Sun, was adopted as a holy day, or holiday, and attendance at the new Christian church on that day was made obligatory. The months of the year, most of which had Roman origins, were probably deemed 'out of bounds' for any changes as a result of Christianity's debt to Rome; Constantine the Great having been so instrumental in permitting the establishment of the Christian Religion. Added to which, as Christianity hadn't arrived in these islands until 597, these were also probably too well established by then to be changed.

Flower names had also been changed and given new

Christian-related ones; e.g. St John's Wort, which was a panacea for just about everything. The day of its traditional harvesting, the day following the summer solstice, Midsummer's Eve - the most dangerous night of the year when demons are abroad - was also renamed St John's Day. The Star of Bethlehem was the new name given to another plant used in herbal remedies, etc. Where change could be implemented, it was, and the old pagan, simply airbrushed out. 'The Truth' had been rewritten, and anything which did remain and did not accord with the new doctrine, 'The New Truth,' was deemed Black, the work of the Devil, Satanic!

On the subject of Satanism, I remember being most surprised to find that it was suggested that this might have originated from an alternative theological interpretation of pre-creation heavenly events; it being derived from a so-called 'Left path', as opposed to the accepted doctrine, the so-called 'Right path'. This implied that in fact it had nothing to do with the old pagan religions at all, but was very much *directly* linked to the then new Christian religion. The difference between the two paths appeared to hang on some theological argument which ran that:- Prior to God making the world and creating mankind, there was a disagreement in Heaven about whether mankind should be born innocent and without Knowledge, which is what God favoured, or be born with Knowledge, which is what Satan, who was the brother of Michael, Archangel Michael that is, and his followers favoured.

I couldn't help but note, that here again there was the mention of twins opposing each other. In one of our history lessons Felicity had told us about the twins, Romulus and Remus, and that Romulus had killed Remus and went on to found the Kingdom of Rome. And of course we had learnt about Cain and Abel, that Cain had killed Abel, and that Cain had moved to 'the land of Nod, on the east of Eden'[18], where he'd

---

[18] Genesis 5:16

built the city of Enoch and founded a line of succession. However, I didn't know that Michael and Satan were also possibly twin brothers. As Michael is always portrayed as slaying Satan, this story seemed to follow in the tradition of the 'one brother killing the other'. Since reading that article in the newspaper offices, I have subsequently learnt that very similar stories occur in several other writings.

The article didn't explain how anyone could possibly know about the so-called Left and Right Paths, bearing in mind that mankind hadn't even been created at this stage! However, ignoring that little detail, apparently God was going to give mankind Knowledge at a later date, though exactly when this was to be doesn't appear to have been specified, but nonetheless had to be the case because God was in favour of His children having children of their own; something which they could not do without Knowledge. Satan saw this as completely illogical, feeling that mankind should be responsible for its own actions from the date of its creation.

Well, apparently God won the argument and magnanimously banished Satan and his followers to Earth, where they became demons; the fallen angels. The article certainly gave the impression that anyone who rocked the Christian Church's boat was branded as a demon! God then created mankind, Adam and Eve, and placed them in a garden, Eden, where He commanded the man, saying, 'Of every tree of the garden thou mayest freely eat: but of the tree of the knowledge of good an evil, thou shalt not eat of it: for in the day that thou eatest thereof thou shalt surely die.'[19] However, God knew full and well that they had to eat of it in order to have the children that He wanted them to have. And when they did just this, He arranged for them to be thrown out of the garden, suffer pain, illness, ageing and death and so on. The end result was that mankind ended up in exactly the same situation after following this route, as decreed by God,

---

[19] Genesis 2: 16 & 17

as he would have done had he been born with Knowledge in the first place, as Satan had suggested. There was no explanation in the article as to why God thought all of this was a good idea. It all seemed unnecessarily contrived and indeed, arguably sadistic, for no purpose whatsoever. So no, unfortunately, that article didn't give any explanation as to why God's so called Right Path was any better than Satan's so-called Left Path. They just appeared to be different routes to the same end.

However, the broad philosophies of the two did appear to be more at odds with each other, with Satanism seeming to be more focused towards the pursuit of knowledge, and the acceptance of responsibility for one's actions, whereas that of the Christian Church being more focused on, if not towards maintaining ignorance, at least retaining control over knowledge, and to treating people as not being responsible for their actions; and hence no doubt, in need of forgiveness? Satanism struck me as having a philosophy of, 'Here is your freedom, do with it as you will,' whereas the Christian Church's philosophy appeared to suggest, 'We know what's best for you and we'll forgive you if you don't step out of line too much'; though no doubt with the unwritten subtext of, 'of course, if you do step out of line too much, we'll have to make an example of you, so as to keep the rest of the herd in line!' and hence being much more oriented towards power and control than the freedom-oriented Satanist approach, which is no doubt why the then new Church and the monarchs of the day favoured it.

Although it didn't occur to me at the time - this is only something that I have thought about later - I am sure I need hardly point out that these two philosophies are still very much with us today. Namely, do we vote for a 'nanny state' which we expect to look after us and which wants to prescribe what we can and can't do, or do we vote for a more, let us call it laissez-faire or liberal approach, where we have the freedom to choose and make our own destinies, and have to look after ourselves? Again, the main distinction between the two appears to be that of 'control'.

The 'nanny state' wants to monitor all aspects of our lives, particularly our misdemeanours, and now, it seems, wishes to store these on a national database, in the form of digital identification, and so exert control over us in almost exactly the same way that the Church previously did with confessions, which believers were tricked into giving by threats of damnation and hellfire if they did not confess. These days we are possibly not as ignorant as we were back in the Middle Ages, and so threats of damnation and hellfire don't work as well as they used to. However, stopping us from getting employment, blocking our credit card, or bank account, because we haven't paid a parking fine, or have used-up our carbon allowance for the year, is but a modern-day version of the same thing. You must conform, you must obey the rules if we are going to be able to look after you, and we will make sure that you do just that whether you like it or not! This very obvious analogy can be extended just a little further by observing that minor medieval misdemeanours, usually relating to sex, of which there were literally hundreds, were punishable by threats of time spent in Purgatory, and this could be mitigated by purchasing an indulgence. These days, minor misdemeanours, many of which relate to motoring, are usually punishable by a fine. What is the difference between a misdemeanour dreamed up by the Church and one dreamed up by the Government or Council? Both are just a created means of extracting money from the man in the street.

The more laissez-faire or liberal approach, does not impose the same restrictions. Life is more of a free-for-all. However," observed Tom with a wry smile, "we will all have noticed that politicians very rarely repeal rules and laws which they were previously opposed to; regulations never get less in number and taxes never go down! However, whereas freedom from constraints is empowering and allows individuals to get on with their lives unfettered by ludicrous red tape and bureaucracy, and so offers freedom to succeed, it also offers the freedom to fail, and in a society wholly of this type, there is no, or only a very minimal, safety net.

It would seem that the only obvious difference between modern-day and pre-creation philosophies appears to be that somewhere along the line, that which was theologically 'right' has become politically 'left' and that which was theologically 'left' has become politically 'right'."

Tom smiled ruefully at his observation before continuing with his story,

"What I couldn't help but notice was that although each religious philosophy was presented as being The Truth, it was all in presentation, as nothing stood out as being the actual truth or correct version, or whatever name you wish to give it. The different sets of facts, stories, versions of events, philosophies, etc., were, it seemed, just that, different. So what was *The Truth*? At that point, I was none the wiser.

The article also highlighted that there were marked differences in attitude towards enjoying this life in the here and now, on this earth. A chap called La Vey of the Satanists was quoted as saying 'Life is the great indulgence - death the great abstinence! Therefore make the most of the here and now! ..... Choose ye this day, this hour, for no redeemer liveth!' which was followed by, 'Since worship of fleshly things produces pleasure there would then be a temple of glorious indulgence .....'[20] both of which appeared to be the complete antithesis of the view taken by the Christian Church, which as well as talking about heaven and redemption, also gives the impression that only self-denial and abstinence are good, that all pleasure and enjoyment are sinful, and that the resulting misery on this earth will be rewarded by paradise in heaven when one is redeemed.

---

[20] Anton Szandor La Vey; Satanic Bible

Whereas I knew that enjoying one's food was considered sinful, I was surprised to read that the sin of Gluttony was not *just* simply categorised as one of the seven deadly sins, but was sub-divided into five separate sub-sections; presumably, so as to eliminate even the slightest possibility that one might actually derive any pleasure from food. Sex was, perhaps needless to say, for reproductive purposes only and certainly not for enjoyment, when it would be classified as a sin; Lust. Apparently, in the Middle Ages, the Church had forbidden sex, even between married couples, on something like a hundred and forty days of the year, and priests had, in order to frighten their flock into going along with this, warned them that children conceived on these so-called holy days would be born leprous, crippled, blind, epileptic or diabolically possessed! And of course, it almost goes without saying that having a day off and putting one's feet up, was also deemed unthinkable; yet another deadly sin, and this time having the name of Sloth. No, there was no doubt at all that the Christian Church of those days did not want one to enjoy this life on this earth. Or alternatively, was it the Church saying, 'we know you are not enjoying this life on earth, but stick with us, continue to believe in our religion and you will be rewarded in the Heaven that awaits you'? So was all of this far more to do with control and power, keeping the man in the street in his impoverished position, and with that, the Church's accumulating of wealth?

This seemed very probable given that many of the Church's minor misdemeanours were deemed venal sins and punishable by time spent in Purgatory, which, as already mentioned, could be reduced by the purchase of an indulgence. Felicity's comments about control, power and wealth being what men desire, and not what the religion itself requires, came back to me, and I wondered how much of all of this was about the actual religion itself and how much was about men using religion as a pretext for their own ends? However, then as now, people either choose to, or are forced to, worship 'that which is presented.' So the 'that which is presented,' be it historical texts and beliefs, or the then current interpretations of same by those in the positions of power at the time, is surely, rightly or wrongly, that which constitutes that religion at that point in time? And it struck me that Felicity's justifications could only be true in hindsight when a new current attitude permitted such views. In which case, are these not just excuses for what was deemed to be perfectly right and proper at the earlier point in time, a bit in the same vein as reclassifying that which had been previously deemed as a fact, as an allegory? 'How many things we held yesterday as articles of faith which today we tell as fables' was how Michel de Montaigne, a 16th century philosopher, had worded this 'shifting of the goalposts.'

However, up to that point, in all the arguments presented for and against the worship of:- Black Magic, Satanism or the Christian Church's God, I had seen no real mention of the word which then caught my eye;

Evil

Yes, there had been mention of God, gods, saints, angels, fallen angels, demons, Satan and so on; all names, or titles, which any one religion might wish to use to enhance its own status and/or put down others; 'We are the true faith! Our deity is a god, yours is a devil!' But most surprisingly there had been no mention, other than in passing in Genesis, of good or evil.

My mind went back again to that memorable R.I. lesson, and the agreement of all that good exists. We know this, can see it and feel it. It may, or may not have anything to do with any god or gods, but there is no doubting that it is a genuinely beautiful thing in itself, which we can and do experience in our lives. And on the opposite pole is evil; the ghastly, the malevolent, the wanton destruction for its own sake; and we know that. The article I was reading then went on to state that some people actually worship it. Yes, worship evil! But strangely, that was all that was said about it. There was no explanation, nothing further to shed any light on why anyone would wish to revere foulness, bestiality, or worship defilement, ruination and darkness. I remember thinking that I couldn't help but feel that as much as the Christian Church, Satanists and Black Magic practitioners, might disagree, and disagree quite profoundly on some things, they all would agree that it should be goodness that was to be revered and that evil, and especially the worship of evil that was to be abhorred.

I remember feeling slightly sick. How could anyone want to do that; worship Darkness? A Darkness, where, as John Milton had worded it, there is 'no light, but rather darkness visible serv'd only to discover sights of woe, regions of sorrow, doleful shades, where peace and rest can never dwell, hope never comes.'[21] Who would want this? An arch devil? A Lucifer? Who could actually want, no, desire this?

---

[21] John Milton, Paradise Lost, Book 1

Chapter 12

Seeds Of Doubt.

When I got home, I remember that I really didn't know what to think, as I was feeling almost more confused than ever. Was what I had read in that newspaper true or not? Was all that occult stuff, and indeed some of that other stuff that I had read about the early Christian Church, just made-up fictitious mumbo-jumbo that made good copy for a newspaper article? Or was it true, actually true? There was no doubting that the journalists had lapped everything up. Throw-in a mention of occult and Black Magic, and a picture of an eccentric-looking old guy with a strange foreign sounding name, and then, if the accompanying picture also contained a shrunken head or two, this was a journalist's dream and the paper was onto a winner! But that doesn't make any of it true. So what was I supposed to make of it? What was *The Truth?*

I decided that the only way I was likely to sort this out was to go and have a chat with someone, but who? Whereas I had toyed with the idea of talking things over with the Thompson twins, but only briefly, as I quickly decided against this on the grounds of, well if I am honest, that they would just laugh at any idea that the school's dead, stuffed wildlife had anything remotely like a genuine Satanic connection, though no doubt Teddy would have loved the idea! 'Have you had too much of your mum's elderberry wine, Tom?' And no, I didn't really want to talk about it with my mother and father either. This subject was rather like sex; who can you trust to talk to seriously about what it is that you want to know, especially when you are so aware that you know almost nothing about it?

Of course the Reverend Bitterling was dead, but I wouldn't have wanted to talk with him about this anyway. He was a narrow-minded bitter little wet fish of a man who appeared to have resented being stuck out in a rural parish and being over-looked for promotion to higher office. I know it sounds unkind to have thought that about him when he had just died - just been killed? - but I'd never liked him, and now I come to think about it, he was probably one of the reasons why I never went to church. However, he did have a new curate, who appeared to be a much nicer guy and so I thought, perhaps I could have a word with him.

So the next day, Sunday, I wandered down to the church in the morning and hung around in the churchyard until the service was over. Oh goodness! It was like going to the dentist. You know that horrible empty feeling that you have in your stomach while you're sitting in the waiting room? Eventually, people started filing out. A 'Hello Tom,' from here, a 'Good morning Thomas,' from there, and a more honest, though almost more embarrassing, 'Hello Tom, what are you doing here?' which was of course the unspoken question behind every other greeting. I almost wished the ground would swallow me up, but the feeling and time passed, and eventually I steeled myself and walked into the church, and straight up to our new curate, the Reverend Money.

"Good morning, sir, if you can spare the time, can I have a word?" I blurted out, all nerves.

"Of course you can," he said cheerily. "If you could help me tidy up these hymn books. Then I'm all yours."

As we collected and stacked up the books, my nerves eased. Afterwards, I realised that that was why he'd asked me to help with the books. When we had finished, others were still busy in the church, so he said to me,

"Shall we go outside? It's Thomas, isn't it?"

"Yes."

"Oh, good. I am gradually getting to know everyone's name,"

he said in an almost conspiratorial manner and then added, "Now, what is it that you wanted to talk about?"

"Will you be our new vicar?" I asked him, still unable to bring myself to voice my concerns.

"I don't know. We'll have to wait and see. Is it the Reverend Bitterling's death that is worrying you, like it is worrying a lot of others?"

"Yes, I suppose so. What with it happening just after Halloween, almost immediately after he'd visited our school."

"Let's have a seat," he said, sitting down on the bench at the base of the church tower and beckoning me to do likewise.

"Yes, one thing did come very quickly after the other, didn't it? So Thomas, or should I call you Tom? What is it that's troubling you?"

I told him about the stuffed animals and birds in the cases that had arrived at the school, and how I had been down to the newspaper offices in the town and what I had discovered there, and then I rather ground to a halt, as I realised that I was going to have to tell him about getting into the school at night and finding that some of the exhibits weren't there.

"So don't tell me," he said, realising that I was having difficulty. "You've done, shall we say, a little bit more detective work? Perhaps checked out this collection at a different time of day?"

How on earth had he guessed that?! And did he notice my embarrassment at hearing this? I wasn't at all sure, but with the benefit of hindsight, of course he must have had a pretty good idea. Everyone knew about Felicity's engagement ring, and he must have known why Bitterling had come and exorcised, or whatever it was he had done to Syphre's dead, stuffed animals and birds. Likewise, he must have heard the rumours and so of course must have known that something was amiss. However, he continued in his easy, slightly conspiratorial manner,

"Don't worry, Tom, it's not a hanging offence," he said with a laugh.

"No, but it might be a caning one," I said in relief at his understanding.

"Ah, yes," he said, looking at me in a knowing way. "Then we had better keep this just between ourselves."

With renewed confidence, I continued.

"Only three cases had been opened; those of the fox, the magpie and the bat, and in each case the occupant had definitely gone. We saw the empty cases."

"We? I don't want to know who was with you, Tom, so don't tell me. Now, you were saying that you saw the empty cases."

Oh goodness! I was cringing inside, realising that I had so very nearly spilt the beans on Teddy and Bobby, and was thankful that Reverend Money had saved me from myself. Although he said nothing more, I felt sure he knew who comprised my 'we' even though he'd said he didn't wish to know. However, I'd said it now, and so there was no going back. From now on it was 'we'.

"Um, yes. When the fox got out, we weren't really sure what happened, because it could have been another fox that had got Dave Parker's dad's chickens, though Renard - Renard's the name on the base of the case - did look better, a bit fatter, had a bit more fur and looked a bit less dead than it did before. But we couldn't be certain that Renard had done it," I tried to explain. "But with the magpie, it was not the same .... I can't think of .... it had to be the bird itself that put Felicity's engagement ring in the case because .... how else could it have got there? It was already there when we looked. We didn't put it there."

"Yes," said a pensive Reverend Money, "I had heard that Felicity had lost her ring and that it had turned up at your school."

"Yeah, the magpie's case had also been opened by someone in our class, just like the fox," I said, being careful not to mentioning Jennifer's name, "It was in the afternoon, when Miss Loveless took us into the film room for a geography slide show. She made a bit of a fuss about it. The jar containing the bat was lifted at the same time, but Miss Loveless didn't see that. We went back to the room at about 8.00 in the evening, and at that time, the ring and the magpie were inside the case. So the magpie must have left the case and returned before then."

"Yes," he said hesitantly. "Or possibly whoever picked up Felicity's ring, perhaps put it in the case before then?"

"But we didn't!" I insisted.

"Tom. I didn't say you did. But it is just possible that someone else might have done so, and that there might just be another explanation."

Up until that point, I had assumed that it was only Teddy, Bobby and I who really knew what had been happening. So if this was not the case, did this mean that someone else, or others, had also been into the school after hours and had also seen what we had? We hadn't told anyone. So how had Reverend Money so easily guessed at what he described as 'a little bit more detective work'? Oh blimey! As he had so easily guessed at this, did it mean that someone else knew that we'd been into the school after hours? I felt a slight shiver of fear and a twinge of guilt as I wondered if we three were going to get hauled up in front of Old Badger on the Monday. And it was with this new worry churning in my head, that I responded to the Reverend Money somewhat unenthusiastically,

"Yes, er, I suppose so."

However, I felt sure that things weren't quite as straightforward and logical as he seemed to be suggesting. Felicity must have known where and when she'd lost her ring. But she obviously hadn't known that it was in the magpie's case until someone had found it there. Had she then discussed the mysterious nature of this with Old Badger and Bitterling? And then, if there was a logical explanation for everything, as Reverend Money was now suggesting and as Old Badger had suggested, why had Bitterling come along to the school, all dressed up in his vicar's garb and with his Bible, crucifix and such like? There had been rumours all around the village, all of which suggested that others, particularly our teachers, must have noticed things as well. So what exactly was it that had prompted Old Badger to ask Bitterling to carry out his exorcism?

I continued trying to explain,

"When we looked, the fox was there and so was the magpie, but the bat wasn't, and now that its jar has broken, it can't come back. It has nowhere to come back to."

"I think we know that there are one or two in your school who would rather like to have a stuffed, dead bat hanging up in their bedrooms, don't we?"

The Reverend Money must have already known of Marianne's predilection for the ghoulish. Embarrassingly, I found myself colouring at the thought of her. Fortunately, he either didn't notice or chose not to, and continued,

"But, yes, Tom, I take your point about the broken jar."

"Yes, it broke, right as he was holding his cross at it," I said, brightening at the prospect that he might be believing me.

"So I heard. But again, Tom, this could just be a coincidence, though in the circumstances I grant you, a slightly strange and mysterious coincidence."

He went on to tell me, "Glass, especially old glass, can just suddenly shatter if it has not been cooled properly; it is all to do with internal stresses in the glass. Have you never seen a bottom fall out of one of your mother's jam jars for no apparent reason? The bell-jar had been moved, hadn't it?"

"But the Reverend Bitterling had gashes to his face and was dead, face down in front of the altar!" I exclaimed, in an almost desperate attempt at trying to hold on to my belief in a supernatural explanation of the events to date, while the Reverend Money appeared to be suggesting possible sensible, logical reasons for just about everything that I had mentioned up to that point.

"True, Tom. But the Reverend Bitterling was not a young man, and we all have to die of something. Don't forget that the jar shattering when it did might have shocked him more than it shocked you; he was right next to it after all. Just imagine that you were standing where he was. How do you think that might have felt? It is not impossible that he died of a heart attack, though we don't know just yet, and as for the gashes on his face, it is always possible that when he fell, his face hit the metal crucifix he was carrying and was gashed by it. Again, we don't know that."

I felt crushed.

"So there was nothing written on the altar cloth either?" I asked, remembering Teddy's rather dramatic offering of the morning after.

"Not that I know of."

So was all that stuff that Teddy had told me about Satanic rites, just another one of his stories, another of Teddy's pranks? I felt a touch cross with him. It was alright to play a prank that had a bit of humour in it, but where was the humour in this? The Reverend Bitterling was dead after all.

"I appreciate that the whole business is a bit mysterious, Tom," continued Reverend Money, "and I am not for a moment saying that the version of events that you have told me is not true. However, I am suggesting that we should be careful not to jump to any conclusions too quickly. Right now, we don't know all the facts, and so there may be other explanations for what has happened. So I suggest we need to keep open minds on this."

Although the Reverend Money appeared to be pouring cold water on what I had said, I had noticed that some of his replies such as, 'Now, you were saying that you saw the empty cases' and 'I take your point about the broken jar,' suggested that he might have more of an open mind than I was giving him credit for and might know more than he was letting on.

This was the first time that I'd had a proper chat with him. Up until then, it had just been introductions and a hello, and I remember that I found myself warming to him. He wasn't your usual priest. Well, he certainly wasn't anything like Bitterling; even his name sounded better! However, he was a bit old to still be a curate. I'd heard that he'd previously had a job in finance, for which his name seemed far more suited, even if the job hadn't suited him, before giving it all up and becoming a priest. Again, with hindsight, it seems reasonable to speculate that because Reverend Money was a bit old for the job he was doing, he and Bitterling had probably got along fairly well, because Bitterling, and certainly Mrs Bitterling, also thought that he (Bitterling) was a bit old for the job he was doing, being just a parish priest that is.

"So do you believe in Black Magic, Satanism and Devil Worship, or is all that just made up?" I asked, feeling that, well, if I couldn't discuss this with him now and get my muddled thoughts sorted out, then I wouldn't be able to discuss it with anyone. In for a penny, in for a pound. This was my chance.

"You like to choose your questions, don't you, Tom?" he said with a smile. "I am a priest don't forget, so you can hardly expect me to believe in Black Magic or Devil Worship. But I think I know what you mean."

I felt a flush of embarrassment as I realised that I should have worded my question better. Fortunately, he wasn't put out in the least, and after a brief pause, continued,

"I am no expert. Indeed, after all your research, you probably know more than I do. But from what you told me earlier, I would say that what you have described was a pretty fair summary."

So, where could I start in order to try and make sense of all that I had read, try and ascertain the truth of it all? To me, Satanism, as described in the article, seemed to be the most reasonable of the religious options, so why didn't the Christian Church believe in this?

"So why do you believe in what you do?" I asked tactlessly.

Reverend Money looked at me with a slightly quizzical expression,

"'To one who has faith, no explanation is necessary. To one without faith, no explanation is possible,'" he replied, with just the hint of a smile.

It was my turn to look quizzically at him, but he went on to explain,

"That was how a thirteenth-century philosopher and theologian, St Thomas Aquinas, explained faith. If you believe Tom, you do, and no explanation is necessary. However, if you don't, then you don't. You can't prove God."

This sounded very similar to the explanation that Felicity had given us in class that day, 'religion is not about proof, it is about belief and faith.' But I couldn't see that. I was wanting some form of proof, some sort of explanation, something tangible, real, something .... oh, I don't know? I wanted *the truth!*

"So what is wrong with having a bit of enjoyment in this life?" I asked, my thoughts dancing back to the descriptions of Satanism, which seemed to advocate this, in contrast to Christianity, which seemed to disapprove of it.

"Nothing."

"So why is the Church so anti-women and always talking of

the nice things in life as being sinful?"

"I am not so sure that the Church is anti-women, as you put it, Tom."

"Then why is there such a problem over women priests? And why are women hardly mentioned in the Bible, and when they are, it is always in derogatory terms and/or in association with whoring and fornication?" I retorted a touch angrily, probably as a result of his having so adeptly kicked all my theories about the stuffed exhibits into touch.

Reverend Money raised an eyebrow at my question, smiled, and then said,

"If I had my way, Tom, I would have women priests tomorrow, but I am not in charge of the Church. Indeed, I am not even in charge here at St Oswald's. Unfortunately, any institution, Tom, whether it be a church, a society, a club, can only be as good as those who are members of it, those who form it and make the rules. And men are not perfect. Even priests are not perfect," he added with the hint of a smile. "Everybody has different views, different opinions."

This was sounding very much like the same argument that Felicity had put forward in class when she and Bobby Thompson had been, er, arguing for and against religion.

"And don't forget that women only got the vote in this country about one hundred years ago, and the Church has been around for two thousand. It takes time for attitudes to change, and they need to change before policy and rules can.

As for whoring and fornication, what can I say? I don't approve of the language either, Tom. It is a bit misogynistic in places, isn't it? It was written by men of course, and as I have just said, men are not perfect. My personal view is that I think that what they were writing about was their own failings, their own weaknesses, and because they were tempted by women, they blamed the women for this rather than blaming themselves, and their use of language results from their disgust at themselves for having been so weak-willed. Does that answer you?"

Well, to be honest, it both did and didn't, though I have to admit that I thought his reply was a bit of a cop out. In other religions I had read that eating, drinking and making merry, as well as sex and sexuality, are looked on positively, as things to be celebrated, things to be enjoyed. Indeed, apparently food and sexually explicit images and sculptures can be seen on and in the temples of other religions, whereas the Church even depicts Adam and Eve, who were supposed to have been born innocent, not looking at all innocent and always modestly covered in fig leaves. Nudity and sexuality are simply not permitted. Indeed, the Adam and Eve story seems to amply illustrate that in the Church's view, sex is not only a cardinal sin, but *the* cardinal sin!

"And the nice things in life are sinful?" ruminated Reverend Money. "You make us sound like a right miserable lot, Tom.

No, I do think a bit of enjoyment is permitted," he said with his usual grin."But it's a question of degree. Didn't I see you eating gob-stoppers at Halloween?"

I nodded, wondering what my eating gob-stoppers had to do with this.

"If you took an entire packet and ate the lot, a) I think you'd be sick, and b) I feel fairly certain that the experience might put you off eating gob-stoppers for a while. It is possible to have too much of a good thing. It is possible to overindulge, or, as we priests say, indulge to excess. OK, right now, I am talking about gob-stoppers, and we both know that eating too many gob-stoppers is only likely to make the person eating them sick. However, indulgence to excess in other things in life can easily end-up harming or hurting others. If parents do exactly as they want, how can they adequately care for their children? It isn't possible to indulge all your desires and fulfil your duty to others at the same time; that is fulfil your duty to those to whom you have a responsibility, and this is especially so in adult relationships.

You mentioned the Bible's unfair treatment of women. However, the so-called 'sins of the flesh' that you were alluding to earlier, are not called sins for nothing. Those sins, as I am certain Mrs Shaw has already explained to you, the sins of coveting another man's wife and of adultery, can wreck a marriage, and not just the lives of the parents, but more importantly, the lives of their children as well. So Tom, I don't think one is being a miserable old so-and-so for warning that it is not good to indulge to excess. Everything in moderation, is probably the best approach, which is certainly *not* the same as saying none at all."

I had to admit that although this sounded pretty reasonable, it certainly didn't tally one hundred percent with what I had read in that newspaper article or with what little I had read in the Bible. And, although Felicity had mentioned the 'sins of the flesh', this had been more in passing; she hadn't actually explained them to us.

So I began to form the impression that the truth, or rather Truth, was not about facts as such, but rather about what one believed them to be; 'To one who has faith, no explanation is necessary. To one without faith, no explanation is possible,' as Reverend Money had said. So is truth what we *believe* to be the case, or is it what we *know* to be the case? And hence, does this mean that if enough people, the majority, say, believe something to be true, then it is so, even if, perhaps, it isn't? The world is flat. The earth is at the centre of the universe, Adam and Eve were made by God and set down in the Garden of Eden. All, true facts?

This did not sound very positive or conclusive to me.

Oh, why couldn't this be easy?

<h1 style="text-align:center"><u>Chapter 13</u></h1>

<u>The Weeks Leading Up To The Winter Solstice.</u>

In the weeks that followed the death of the Reverend Bitterling, everyone was nervous and ill at ease. At school, Old Badger dealt with assembly quickly and then rushed off and locked himself in his study where he seemed to remain all day. Miss Loveless, who had taken to wearing tight-fitting polo-neck jumpers and a knee-length skirt now that the weather had gone cold, sat on her desk facing the class, fiddling nervously with a thread on one cuff and crossing and recrossing her legs, much to the delight of Teddy Thompson who sat in a first row desk. The days were getting shorter, and with the dark evenings then upon us, no-one hung around after school as all were anxious to get the journey home over with and get indoors as quickly as possible. There was no appetite for the previously popular after-school film shows, and I don't think we saw one that term. Walking around in the dark had completely lost its appeal. The hours of darkness were no longer hours for relaxation at the end of the day, but had become hours of anxiety, when you needed to be indoors, with the windows closed and the lights on. No one mentioned the bat, but there was no doubting that it was on everyone's mind, its tiny black wings casting a huge, dark shadow over our village.

And it was against this background that we heard the dreadful news one afternoon that Felicity's new husband, Aidan, had been killed in an accident; the tractor he was driving had turned over on him. Quite how this had happened wasn't at all clear. He was an experienced driver, was not the sort of man to take risks, knew the area he was working on like the back of his hand, and so everyone was at a total loss to comprehend how this appalling accident had happened. Although he also had gashes to his face, it was not easy to say whether these were suspicious and caused by something other than the accident itself, as he was pretty badly damaged, having been crushed under the full weight of the tractor. But this didn't stop rumours from circulating. Indeed, even at his funeral I heard a few wild speculations being passed around. However, I noticed that both Bobby, and more particularly Teddy, who was more inclined towards setting a rumour in train, were respectfully quiet and not involved in any of this.

Poor Felicity was devastated. She and Aidan had only been married a few months, and although we kids didn't know it at the time, she was pregnant, with, as we learned later, twin girls.

The day of Aidan's funeral dawned damp with a leaden foggy sky touching the tops of the trees, which stood there silently, still and heavy with the previous night's rain, dripping like a row of rotting corpses in the Stygian gloom. Death seemed to pervade the valley; cold, still, damp, death. Even the only discernible movement was also that associated with death; the barely perceptible shifting of thin vertical wisps of cloud, which rose up between the more distant conifers like shrouds or wraiths before gradually fading and disappearing.

Because of Felicity's connections with both the village and the school, Old Badger closed the school for the morning so that we all could attend the funeral service at St Oswald's, and as a result of this and the fact that just about the entire village attended, the church was absolutely packed. Reverend Money conducted the service. Although he, in consultation with Felicity, had chosen positive, life-affirming and uplifting hymns and prayers, it was still a sad affair. As I have already mentioned, Aidan and Felicity were newly married, young, just starting a family, and so had so much of life to look forward to. For this promise of a future to be so cruelly smashed in this untimely manner struck everyone as awfully unfair.

Indeed, now I think about it, that was probably the first time that it really hit me that life wasn't fair, that dreams and hopes for the future could be there one minute and lay in broken pieces on the ground the next. What type of God could permit this, permit life and happiness to be so casually snuffed out? Wasn't He supposed to be omnipotent and so have infinite power over the evils of the world? Almost inevitably, my mind went back to that R.I. lesson and Felicity's rock solid belief that God would look after her. It didn't look like He was doing so to me. Perhaps she felt differently. Perhaps she felt that He had looked after her and that He was continuing to do so. But how could this be, when there could be no doubt that her life would never be the same again without Aidan, the man with whom she had chosen to share it? Losing Aidan must have felt like loosing a part of herself. And what of their twin girls who would grow up never knowing their father? I just couldn't help but wonder where that left Felicity's belief that she and hers would be protected? And would she gain some sort of consolation from believing that He was 'there to carry us through when the odds seem stacked against us, even in our darkest moments when there appears to be no hope,' as she had said to us on that day? I had no idea, and I am afraid couldn't reconcile any of this. There was just way too much doubt for me.

So now the village had two unusual and unexpected deaths to come to terms with, and if this wasn't enough, there was yet more to come.

However, the next piece of unexpected news was nothing like as terrible as the aforementioned, and came about a couple of weeks before Christmas when Teddy told me that he and his brother and the entire Thompson family were leaving to go to Australia. Their parents had decided to take advantage of the £10 ticket offer that the Australian government was offering at the time, and so they were all off to a new life 'down under'. Judging from the way he told me this news, Teddy was obviously looking forward to it. So this would be their last term with us. As much as they were a pair of scallywags - as described by my mother - they were my best friends, good fun, and we'd had some great times together, so I knew that I would miss them.

Then, on the very afternoon of the last day of term, another appalling event occurred; Sheila Simonds disappeared. Yes, I know it sounds impossible, a girl can't just disappear, but she did. The weather was blowing a gale outside our classroom, and in the strong gusts you could feel the hut moving and creaking. Sheila was with us in class one minute and then had obviously gone out of the room without saying anything, so no one, not even her close friends had any idea of where she had gone, and then, quite simply, she didn't come back. She was the class monitor that week, in charge of ensuring that we all had pencils and pens, and that our ink wells were topped up, and so, with hindsight, it was perfectly possible that she had gone off to the store room in the film-hut to attend to one of these tasks, but no-one thought of that at the time. Indeed, to start with, no-one thought anything was amiss, and it was only after she had been gone for about half an hour that some started asking where she was.

"Now, you girls, will you stop talking and get on with your work. School is not finished yet," said Miss Loveless in a stern schoolmarmish voice.

"But Miss," said Jennifer, "Sheila is not here, Miss."

"What do you mean, not here?" said Miss Loveless looking around the class.

"She was here before playtime, but she's not here now," replied Jennifer.

"Oh?"

"But her coat is still on the rack, Miss," said another of the girls.

"Well, does anyone know where she has gone?"

No one did.

"Everyone, remain seated, and carry on with your work," and with that, Miss Loveless left the room.

A minute or so later, she returned with Old Badger.

We were told to get our coats on and go and look around the school. However, by then it was beginning to get dark, had started to rain, and the wind was still as strong as ever. We all wandered around calling, 'Sheila!' at the tops of our voices, but the wind just carried our cries away into the gathering gloom. I think Old Badger realised pretty quickly that using us kids to try and search for a missing girl in fading light and deteriorating weather was not only hopeless, but also potentially dangerous. So, not wanting to be held responsible for giving us all hypothermia, he called the whole thing off and sent us home early.

By the time I got home, it was well and truly dark, so I could clearly see the flashing bright blue lights of the police cars across the fields when they arrived at the school. Then I saw torch beams both scanning across the fields, moving about on them and going along the edges of them, and so guessed that men were going up and down the hedgerows. The beams of light then moved off towards the river. When the wind let up, I could hear the occasional bark of a dog, and so I guessed that the police had dogs with them, but, as by then it was absolutely chucking it down with rain, it seemed unlikely that they would be able to pick up anything like a scent trail.

I looked out at the night; a pitch black maelstrom of wind and rain, and shivered; not from the physical cold, the house was nice and warm, but from the horror of what had already happened and appeared to be still happening. Before the breaking of the bat's bell-jar things were just strange, weird even, but after that they had taken a turn, a very unpleasant and serious turn; people had started dying. Bitterling had died just a few hours afterwards right in front of the altar in his church. Aidan had been crushed to death beneath a tractor on his farm, and now Sheila Simonds was missing. Would we find her dead tomorrow? Her parents must have been worried sick. What a thing to happen just before Christmas.

The bat was out there. Out there somewhere, wandering the night sky, unable to return to its jar and so like a soul in limbo, neither in heaven or hell, damned? Damned and fated to fly the night sky forever, wreaking .... ? Yes, wreaking what? What had it already done? What more would it do to 'the people which sat in darkness' and the 'shadow of death'?[22] And why? Why?

Later, I checked my diary and found that it was the day of the Winter Solstice; the shortest day of the year.

After we had finished supper and I was helping my mum to clear the dishes away, she suddenly said,

"Looks as if someone is having a bonfire at your school."

"Well, no one told us."

We both took a better look.

"That's not a bonfire," exclaimed my mother, "your school is on fire!"

---

[22] Matthew 4:16

Chapter 14

Fire!

If you ask most boys, they'll tell you that they hate their school, but when you see yours going up in flames, you realise that perhaps you don't, or rather didn't hate it quite as much as you thought you did. After all, it has been the focus of your life up until then. You've met your friends there and continue to meet them there on a daily basis. Many of your activities are centred on it. You don't actually dislike all the teachers. Indeed, some you have known almost all your life, like Felicity for example, and are not only quite nice, but almost like second parents. Like it or not, the school forms one of the hubs of the village, rather like the church and the pub, and the school especially so for the kids. So yes, when you see yours going up in flames, you realise that it does have a special place in your heart after all.

"Can I go and see?" I asked my mother.

"Be careful. Don't get too close," she replied.

I grabbed a torch and stepped into my Wellington boots and ....

"Thomas, your jacket!"

Although the torrential rain of an hour or so previously had almost stopped and the wind had eased, there was still a bit of drizzle in the air.

"Yes, mum." I kicked off my boots, went and found my jacket, and thirty seconds later, with boots back on again, was running across the field.

By the time I'd arrived, the fire had really taken hold. It was the old film-room hut that was alight, and when I arrived, it was almost completely gutted. The huts nearest to it were also well ablaze. The police were already there, no doubt, because they were still involved in the search for Sheila and so hadn't really left the area. The fire brigade however, still hadn't arrived. I looked around to see who else was there and saw Teddy sitting on a wall with an old coat around his shoulders and being comforted by David's mother. Bobby was with Bill's parents, talking to a policeman. Oh goodness! I thought, what have they been up to? This is not their doing, is it? The Thompson twins swansong; to burn down the school! However, as I walked over towards Teddy, I realised that this couldn't be the case. Teddy was in tears and shaking. David's mother had her arm around his shoulders.

"Hello Thomas," she said as I arrived. "Edward has had a dreadful shock. Could you stay with him for a minute, while I go and see what is happening?"

"She's in there. I think she's in there," sobbed Teddy.

"Who is, dear?" asked David's mother.

"Sheila," mumbled Teddy.

"Oh my God! Stay there, Thomas! Look after Edward. I'll be right back." And with that she ran off in the direction of Bill's parents, Bobby and the policeman.

"Blimey, Teddy! What's happened?"

Even in the light of the flames, I could see that he was ashen-faced. He was shaking and although he was looking in my direction, I got the feeling that he didn't actually see me, as his eyes were just staring blankly at nothing. It was pretty obvious that something dreadful had happened.

"Teddy?"

"She's mad. Completely mad," he sobbed staring at the burning building.

Poor Teddy, he was half-crying, as if he had cried his lot and had no more tears in him, but still had the need to cry more. I'd never seen Teddy like this before. Indeed, I'd never seen anyone like this before. Teddy had always been so confident, cocky even, so sure of himself, so irrepressible, but there he was huddled in an old coat which was far too big for him, looking almost literally, half his former self.

"What happened, Teddy? Who's mad?"

He turned his head and looked at me through red, sore eyes.

"We decided - you know we're going off to Aus., Tom? We decided to have one last look round. We came through the fence," he explained half-beckoning with his arm, "just as we did that night" (presumably meaning the night when he, Bobby and I had come in to check if the fox was in its case).

However, as he then went on to explain, when they'd got half-way across the playground, suddenly the whole place lit up. Initially, they'd thought someone had seen them and had switched on the lights, but it wasn't that, it was as a result of someone slashing through one of the blackout blinds with a knife! The major part of that blind had suddenly collapsed and had hung down one side of the window frame, rendering it totally useless as a blackout. It was only then that they realised that all the blinds in the room had been down and that the room was not unoccupied, but very much the opposite. They also didn't grasp immediately that the light shining out onto the playground, wasn't electric light, but was fire light and that a major part of the room was ablaze.

With a faltering voice punctuated with violent sobs, Teddy went on to explain that to start with, they couldn't really make out what was going on, but did see that the fronts of all the display cases to the zoological specimens were open and that the glass bell-jars had been taken off all their long dead inhabitants.

"Those stuffed, so-called zoological specimens, they weren't there for us Tom. They were there for her, for her insane Witches Sabbaths!"

"Her?! Who?"

"Loveless, Tom. Who do you think?"

Louise Loveless?

Insane Witches Sabbaths?

Our class teacher?!

I just couldn't believe this, and so it was somewhat distantly that I heard Teddy saying how he and Bobby had seen her alternately stabbing at the floor with a huge knife and then, for no apparent reason, flailing it dementedly around her head. It all sounded so totally bizarre, so totally unreal, that I really wasn't sure whether I had understood Teddy correctly or, if as a result of his shock, he had completely lost it. And when he went on to describe how Loveless had been wearing a long white semi-transparent nightdress, I was convinced the latter was the case!

"She must have been naked under this diaphanous robe thing that she had on, as we could see the silhouette of her naked body through it, backlit by the flames."

Was this some bizarre erotic fantasy of Teddy's or ....? But it didn't seem like it; Teddy's almost expressionless voice, so unusual for him, and his huddled, frightened-looking appearance, suggested that this was not one of his games.

"The sleeves were soaked in blood, Tom," he continued, "and she had what looked like a lyre on her head, only it wasn't a lyre, it was two large curved horns. She looked like .... like a devil, Tom!"

'And I beheld another beast coming up out of the earth; and he had two horns ....'[23]

---

[23] Revelation 13:11

Teddy gasped a couple of times, his body shaking, and then continued.

"Then we saw what she was swiping at with the knife. It was the bat!" he blurted out.

"The bat was in the room with her?" I asked, surprised at hearing this revelation.

However, according to Teddy, it seemed that although it was in the room with her, it was most certainly not with her in her endeavours. Indeed, quite the opposite appeared to be the case, as it was apparent that the bat was so clearly attacking her; it was flying at her head, and she was trying to fend it off with the knife.

"You should have seen it, Tom. It was amazing," Teddy said, with a hint of awe and excitement in his voice.

"The bat was amazing at flying! There was Loveless flailing about with this massive knife thing, and the bat just flipped its wings and the huge blade just carved harmlessly through the air. She never got nowhere near it!"

"And then she'd stab at the floor again," he said, in a more subdued voice, while trying to stifle another sob. "There was obviously .... obviously something there, Tom .... but we couldn't see what."

He went on to describe the fire continuing to increase in its intensity with further blinds catching light as the flames licked higher and spread around the room. However, it had seemed that both Loveless and the bat were completely oblivious of this as they continued their bizarre fight; the bat relentlessly continuing to harry Loveless, while she was attempting to fend it off with the knife, but unable to touch it.

"We knew she was weird, but not this weird!" said Teddy, his voice rising with indignation.

"Knew she was weird?"

"Oh, come on, Tom. Wakey, wakey! Yes, weird. She has a name like Loveless, yet she has probably had sex with half the men in the valley."

"What?!"

"You didn't know?" he said quietly, obviously genuinely surprised at my ignorance and went on to describe how just about every night when he and Bobby had visited the little car-park in the woods, the cinder one, opposite the turning for Burnhope Farm, she was in the back of someone's car, one leg akimbo over the back of one of the front seats and the car bouncing up and down on its springs. Why did I think she looked so tired all the time? Apparently, they'd even seen her with Old Badger one evening.

"Blimey!"

"She was after just about anything in trousers, Tom. She wasn't fussy, just permanently randy."

Goodness! I felt as if my world was being turned upside down, as if I had spent the past term living in some parallel universe, as I'd known nothing about this. But, as I sat there stunned at this latest revelation, I heard echoes of my conversation with Reverend Money that day; phrases such as 'indulgence to excess', 'sins of the flesh' and 'men - so presumably women as well - without joy becoming addicted to carnal pleasures,'[24] and so as much as Teddy's story sounded so totally unbelievable, for some strange reason, it didn't sound completely impossible.

"But what happened in the room, Teddy?" I asked, trying to get a grip of myself and come to some sort of terms with what I'd just learned.

---

[24] "Man cannot live without joy; therefore when he is deprived of true spiritual joys it is necessary that he become addicted to carnal pleasures." St Thomas Aquinas.

"She was nothing like she was in class, Tom .... She was completely mad! .... Insane, demented! .... Like someone possessed!

That red hair of hers was flying in all directions.

Her face .... Oh! It looked dreadful! No, no, I don't mean, what with all the blood on it. I mean, her face was dreadful to look at .... dreadful! It had changed, Tom. Completely changed. Like she was like a different person .... as though .... almost not human at all .... like a mad .... a mad devil!"

He went on to describe wide, wild, flaming eyes and a mouth wide open like that of a rabid dog, with thin, almost purple lips drawn back and white fangs exposed as she screamed at the bat as it swooped down on her yet again.

Then he described how their fight was like watching a diminutive, ugly, black, leathery angel Puriel fighting a giant, terrifying, white-clad, blood-soaked she-devil, with neither combatant appearing to being prepared to give up as the fire raged inexorably about them.

And as I listened to Teddy's faltering description, it hit me; isn't it strange how we sometimes get things so completely and utterly wrong, jump to completely the wrong conclusion, only to find out that in fact it is the exact opposite which is true? 'Everything we hear is an opinion, not a fact. Everything we see is a perspective, not the truth.' [25] There we had all been assuming that it was the bat that had been responsible for all the dreadful happenings of the past few months, and that it was the bat that was to be feared, and yet now, it seemed that the absolute opposite was the case, and that the ugly little moth-eaten, black leathery thing was in fact the 'good guy', the one who was 'on the side of the angels', and was there in the burning film room fearlessly and selflessly battling with evil, battling with an evil being vastly larger than itself!

---

[25] Marcus Aurelius.

My mind flashed back to the shattering of the glass bell-jar and I remembered that I, probably like everyone else, had judged the likely cause of this by the effect it had had on Reverend Bitterling, and in fairness to him, he must have felt that this was due to some malevolent force; but just suppose the opposite was true, that the shattering of the glass was the breaking of whatever hold Loveless had exerted on the bat? 'Please children, leave the cases closed' was something she had said and said in a manner that, now I thought about it, was way more insistent than necessary, on more than one occasion. Was she somehow holding the dead exhibits captive? With its glass bell-jar broken, the bat had no prison to return to. It could remain free; free to act. Did Loveless realise this? In which case no wonder she had been so nervous after the so-called exorcism, as she must have known that the shattering of that jar would have broken her hold over the bat, thus releasing it from her control. No doubt, in her panic, she had stupidly focused on that useless priest Bitterling, because she saw him as damaging her plan, even though he presented no danger to her. And no wonder she was now fighting like one possessed; she could not let the bat win, as those flames would not just burn down the building, but burn her soul and purge all that they consumed. She was fighting for her very existence!

But why was she in the film room in the first place? What was she doing there, and precisely what madness was going on in there? Was she enacting some bizarre, insane ritual, something to do with her trying to regain control of, what was for her, a lost situation? Whatever it was, it had certainly brought the bat back, and back with a vengeance! This most definitely would not have been her intention, as the bat appeared set on her destruction. Indeed, had it been freed for that singular purpose? Had Bitterling's exorcism actually worked? And although none of us had realised at the time, had Bitterling realised this when the jar shattered, realised that evil was real and present, and so was his shock due to this realisation? And was the bat now fulfilling its task, the task for which it had been set free, even if it meant sacrificing its own life? However, Teddy's description of events suggested that this, the sacrificing its own life, appeared extremely unlikely, as Loveless seemed totally incapable of touching it with the knife, let alone harming it. This was a fight that Loveless was not going to win; it was, so obviously, just a case of when she would lose.

And then it happened. She stabbed at the floor yet again, and as she straightened up the bat shot at her face, its claws spread wide, and one tore a long gash down one of her cheeks. Loveless screamed in pain, her lips thin, stretched and pulled back, revealing gums, spittle and teeth. She raised a blood soaked hand to the torn and bleeding flesh, whilst with the other she slashed wildly at the bat with the knife, but too wildly, as she lost her balance and it seemed almost as if in slow motion, she toppled back over a desk, which must have been serving as a makeshift altar as it still had a chalice and a lit candle standing on it, her arms flying upwards mirroring the lyre-shape of the horns on her head, an accursed being, a damned soul, and she fell screaming into the all-consuming pit of flames! Screaming into the fires of Hell!

Within a few short seconds, the remaining blinds had caught light, the glass in the windows cracked and blew out, and the whole hut became a raging inferno. It was at this stage that the police, who had obviously gone off to have a meal and warm-up a bit after the appalling weather of earlier that evening, arrived hurriedly back on the scene, and people from the village started arriving. Teddy said it was shortly after that, that I'd arrived. I looked up and saw that an ambulance had stopped on the road. One of the medics came over with Bill's mother and collected Teddy, who presumably went off to the hospital. That was the last time I saw him. I only realised after he'd gone that I never really said goodbye properly to either him or Bobby. That evening robbed us of that.

Chapter 15

The Aftermath.

The following morning was yet another miserable December day. In place of the wind and rain, was a still, cold, raw day with a low grey sky which blanked out the sun, thus preventing it from clearing the mist which hung in the trees, or thawing the blanket of frost that covered the ground. Frost-plastered dead vegetation stood still and silent in front of cold, lifeless drystone walls. Leafless branches of trees hung motionless under the weight of their frozen coating. All was quiet and still, embalmed and padded with frost and mist, as if it were a vast corpse in a white silk-lined coffin.

Death was still very much with us.

Viewed from the roadside, our old school looked pretty much the same as always. However, viewed from across the field, it was a scene of devastation. The odd length or two of charred black timber still stood pointing skyward like strange thin memorials projecting from the frost-free, black mass of ash which lay between two rows of brick plinths upon which had sat the film-room. The whole room and everything in it, all those stuffed exhibits, zoological specimens, or whatever they were, and their cases were gone, had been consumed by the previous night's fire. An odd wisp of smoke or steam rose from the dark heap.

It didn't take long for the police and fire people to discover the burnt, almost cremated remains of two females - one middle-aged woman and one young girl - in the burnt out ruins. We stood on the road and watched silently as the men brought out the two black bags and placed them in the ambulance, though it was obvious to all that the ambulance and its cargo would not be going to the hospital. I saw the Reverend Money talking with Sheila's distraught parents, but the next time I looked in their direction, they'd all gone.

The adjacent classroom was in little better condition than the film-room, and although the other huts didn't look damaged from the road, many in fact were, as a result of the heat. It was inconceivable that we could continue to use the school, not that any of us would have wished to after what had happened, and later in the new year, we learned that we'd been allocated places in another school further down the valley, and that a bus would be laid on to collect us in the morning and bring us home again in the afternoon.

If Sheila's death, the burning of our school and Teddy's bizarre story weren't big enough shocks to come to terms with, when I read the newspaper report on what had happened, I got a further one, as according to that report Miss Louise Loveless was a heroine, who'd suddenly realised that Sheila might be trapped in the store room and had selflessly entered the burning hut to rescue her!

Where on earth had they got this story from? This was nothing like what Teddy had told me that evening. However, it wasn't until just a little later that I started to wonder what Teddy and Bobby had told the police that evening, as it was only then that I realised that they couldn't possibly have told them the same story that Teddy had told me, as they would never have been believed. So was it they, Teddy and Bobby, who had made up the story that I had read in the newspaper? And then, of course, there was the usual nagging doubt about the veracity of anything that you might have heard from Teddy. Had he just spun me a yarn that evening, just for the fun of it? But to spin such a yarn when tears were running down his ashen face, seemed unlikely. So had the pair of them spun a yarn to the police, confident enough in the knowledge that they would be away in Australia, or at least out of the country in a day or so's time, and so safely away from any repercussions that might arise? However, they needn't have worried, because to my knowledge there was no police follow-up, and neither did the newspaper subsequently print anything even vaguely similar to Teddy's tale of events. So what exactly had happened? What was the truth of that evening? I thought I knew, but now suddenly, I wasn't so sure.

When I next met the Reverend Money there was six inches of snow on the ground. It was January and winter was well and truly with us.

"Hello, Tom. Did you have a good Christmas?"

"Yes, thanks."

"And how are you getting on in your new school?"

"Fine," I said somewhat unenthusiastically, because it just wasn't the same as the old one. It struck me that it wasn't just poor Sheila Simonds who had died, the old school had also died, and so too had our childhood innocence. The world was now a different place. My two best friends were now in Australia, or heading towards it, and no longer around. They had gone from my life. The school that I'd shared with them and with others, was no more. It was also gone. I felt alone and cold, and for the first time felt that a whole part of my life was now firmly in the past, was now in the realm of 'memories'. What had happened to those earlier carefree summer days, or the larking about at Halloween? Were they really the days of just a few months ago? Had they actually been a part of *my* life, or were they a part of a dream that I'd had? The world had changed, had suddenly become a cruel, heartless place, where any happiness didn't last, where friends were not there forever, where people died. Had I eaten of the apple without realising it and been forced to leave Eden, and now could no longer go back, no longer go back to what had been?

Reverend Money, whom I already knew had been ordained as our new vicar, steered us to St Oswald's, where we went inside and sat on a pew.

"Did you read the newspaper report on the fire at our school?"
I asked.

"Yes, I did," he replied.

"Is it true? Is that what happened?"

"It sounds as if you don't think so, Tom," he said in a manner,
which I took to imply that possibly he wasn't so certain either.

"So what do you think happened?" he asked.

"I don't know. Yes, we all knew Sheila was the class monitor
that week, and so could have been in the storeroom. The huts
had been creaking in the wind that day, and so it was possible
that the door to the storeroom had become jammed when she
was inside, and she couldn't get out. But why had no-one
thought to look for her in there earlier? It's odd now I think
about it. We were all sent outside to look for her and then were
all sent home. No one, not even the police, looked for her inside
the school."

Had Loveless locked her in so that ....? but I let that thought
hang, not wishing to continue with such a horrible idea and
instead recalled my earlier conversation with Reverend Money
about the strange nocturnal habits of the stuffed zoological
specimens and my researches into pagan beliefs, Satanism, the
early Christian Church and so on, and remembered that he'd
listened and although he'd offered alternative explanations to
the events I'd described, he hadn't dismissed them as totally
stupid or impossible, and so I decided to tell him what Teddy
had told me that evening.

He listened but didn't comment. Even when I'd finished, he
still didn't say anything, and we sat there silent in the stillness
of the church until I asked,

"They were hers, weren't they?" I meant the 'zoological
specimens'.

He nodded his head slowly, but didn't say anything. Was this

his way of confirming what Teddy had told me that night? I wasn't sure. I wasn't sure of anything.

"And I suppose the old school's film-room with its blackout curtains, was obviously ideal for her purpose?" I continued, though I have subsequently wondered as to what her purpose really was; to create darkness during the day and present darkness at night, so as to both literally and metaphorically make darkness visible? Of course, the signs had been there. They had been there from day one, but she was a beautiful, charming, vivacious, sexy woman and so we had all chosen not to see them. The bat, on the other hand, was small, black, leathery, ugly and of course dead, and so hence a so-much-more-appropriate target to pin blame on. White, beautiful and lively is good; black, ugly and dead is bad. It's nice and simple that way. Simple to cling to our preconceptions, our prejudices, select and interpret our evidence to justify our illogical preconceived stance, while all the time refusing to believe that we could, could have just got it all so wrong.

"And she was our teacher. She was supposed to be an example to us .... supposed to be responsible for us," I mumbled.

So why had she chosen to be a teacher? Was it just because schools tend to have a room with blackout curtains where she could store her foul props? But she had no guarantee of that. Or was it that a classroom was a good hunting ground for victims? Oh goodness. Poor Sheila. She was a silly girl, but she didn't deserve that; no-one did. And how many more had there been before Loveless had arrived at our school, and that we knew nothing about? An empty numbness seemed to be growing inside me. Were Loveless' motives that straightforward; simple convenience and bloodlust, or were they deeper, more long-term in nature; locating and indoctrinating recruits, disciples even? But to take innocent children and deliberately corrupt them and lead them into a world of darkness. It was horrific to contemplate, less dramatic but almost more horrific than the story that Teddy Thompson had told me that evening. And as I thought of that, his descriptions of those scenes came crashing back into my mind. The demented madness. The rising and falling knife. The blood over hands, arms and clothing. The wanton excess in all things. The insane, unbridled evil. And she, she in charge of children!

"Yes, that is true," replied Reverend Money, while I, so lost in my rambling thoughts, had all-but forgotten why he was saying this. Oh yes, it was in response to my, 'she was our teacher and was supposed to be responsible for us.'

The horror of it filled me. If what Teddy had described was true, how could someone wish to kill, deliberately kill, an innocent school girl just as a part, only as a part of some ludicrous ritual? It was sickening to think that a life, a young innocent life, had been taken solely for some lunatic religious purpose, and in this case solely for the purpose of some warped desire to worship evil, worship evil for its own sake.

But hold on! Was this actually any different to any of the other mad killings that go on in this world? It wasn't only the likes of Loveless who killed innocents. As Bobby had so succinctly pointed out to Felicity that day, just about all the main religions in the world have done exactly the same in the name of that which they chose to worship. One could easily argue that at least Loveless had had the honesty to dress up in some ludicrous attire and, as openly as is possible in any society, worship the madness in which she believed, as opposed to hypocritically talking of love and tolerance, before commencing to slaughter those who did not worship the same god, or hold with precisely the same religious doctrine.

'How can we live in harmony? First, we need to know we are all madly in love with the same God,' is how Reverend Money's St Thomas Aquinas had put it, and that was back in the twelfth century. We don't appear to have learnt much between then and now. What has been done, and what is so terrible is what is *still* being done in the name of religion. Was

Loveless any worse, any worse than the zealots of the past, the Kings and Popes, or more recent religious fanatics, all of whom appear to think that their god has given them some divine right to either kill, or order others to kill? And what of arrogant Prime Ministers and Presidents who think that they know better than the citizens of a foreign country how they should run their lives and then, through military force, try to impose their values on them?

Reverend Money's other St Thomas Aquinas quotation came back to me, 'To one who has faith, no explanation is necessary. To one without faith, no explanation is possible,' and it struck me how this simple and innocuous sounding homily could also be applied to the most atrocious acts perpetrated in the name of some religion or misguided belief; those who 'believe' require no explanation for their madness and wanton destruction, and those who don't, can't and never will understand the illogical lunacy of those who do.

Yes, Loveless was a dreadful, sick individual in one small village, our village, and so her actions directly touched us, but was she worse than those who callously order the slaying of thousands, knowing full well that many of them will be total innocents? 'Caedite eos. Novit enim Dominus qui sunt eius' ('Kill them all. For the Lord knows His own.') is reportedly what Papal Legate Arnaud-Amaury replied when asked how to differentiate between Cathars (the heretics) and Catholics (the true believers) when Béziers was sacked during the Albigensian Crusades. Possibly our language is not quite so crude these days and euphemistic phrases such as 'collateral damage' and 'for the greater good' are used instead, but is the sentiment really any different?

What is wrong with men? Why can't they just live their lives and leave others alone?

When we each taste of the apple, do we also each eat the worm of evil that has burrowed into it? Why the need to try and control others, to tell them what they should and should not believe, tell them who or what they should and should not worship, and tell them how they should and should not live their lives? Of course, the rot didn't start with Moses and that golden calf. He wasn't the first to show a lack of tolerance and ignore the, in the circumstances, perhaps inappropriately named, Mosaic Law which states 'Whatever is hurtful to you, do not do to any other person.' And how many have subsequently ignored the Biblical, 'Do unto others as you would have them do unto you.'[26], *and especially* when it comes to the beliefs and religions of others? Where is tolerance, love and understanding? Oh why can't people just mind their own business and leave others alone?!

I felt so sick and depressed that I had to pause for a moment before I asked somewhat speculatively, having I hoped, put two and two together correctly,

"Her name wasn't Loveless, was it?"

"No, it wasn't. Her forename was Louise ...." Yes, I noticed that he, a priest, didn't in this instance use the term 'Christian name' "…. but no, her surname wasn't Loveless, it was Syphre, the same as her father's."

"Maximillian Syphre was her father?"

So she was his daughter; Louise Syphre.

By that time, I was feeling numb enough inside so that this latest revelation didn't surprise me anything like as much as it might have done. It was just yet another piece of this bizarre story that I had not known. But if her name was Syphre, why had she chosen to be known as Loveless? Was this how she felt about herself? Unloving, incapable of giving love to another, and so, feeling that none could or would give love to her? What was that St Thomas Aquinas quotation? 'Man, and so presumably woman as well, cannot live without joy; therefore

---

[26] Matthew 7:12

when he, or she, is deprived of true spiritual joys it is necessary that he, or she, become addicted to carnal pleasures'? And if Teddy's observations of her excessive sexual night-time activities in the small cinder car-park were true, had these been motivated by some desperate desire to try and grasp love, a notion that the sex act itself was love, and hence, when this failed to provide that which she so desperately craved, the only logical reason could be that she had not indulged enough and that more was required, and it could/would only be when she'd had enough that her craving for love would be satisfied?

With hindsight, there was no doubting that there had been no joy in her life. Indeed, her life now appeared to have been lonely, empty, futile and devoid of any warmth, any caring - no wonder she and Felicity had not seen eye to eye - and this realisation almost had me feeling sorry for her, almost, that is until I reminded myself that she didn't die alone in that classroom. Her life had only been about taking, using, exploiting. Yes, without love, love-less.

"Did you know that she and Felicity didn't get on?" I asked.

"Yes, I had heard that they weren't the best of friends."

"So did she take Felicity's ring just out of spite? And then deliberately kill Aidan so as to deprive Felicity of her happiness, because she was jealous and unable to find happiness and contentment herself?"

Oh, goodness, Loveless was sick.

The Reverend Money said nothing.

However, life is not just Fate, nor for that matter, is life just Free Will, it is a mixture of both. We can choose, and Loveless, though as I now knew her, Syphre, had been free to choose, even if, possibly, Fate had dealt her a bad hand.

And my thoughts continued to randomly tumble on.

Unlike her, Loveless, Syphre, or whatever her name was, I

was not unloved. So why did I feel so numb and cold, feel so on the outside of everything; feel so excluded? I knew I hadn't deliberately or knowingly eaten of any forbidden fruit; surely those apples in the vicarage garden didn't count? Don't be stupid, Tom, of course Bitterling's apple tree wasn't the Tree of Knowledge! So, if that tree wasn't The Tree, how had I somehow eaten of the metaphorical one without realising it, and had started to feel the effects of pain, loss, and if not ageing, at least the early effects of getting older, had been introduced to death and the madness and evils of the world? Oh, I wanted, so wanted to be back in Eden again, but I knew there was no way back. It was cold out here in this world beyond childhood.

Yes, some things could be answered by being cerebral and rational, like Bobby Thompson, but life wasn't rational. Indeed, it appeared to be anything but! So yes, one did need something to counter the irrational, the illogical, the random nature of things, and I began to grasp what Felicity had said that day; 'but religion is not about proof, it is about belief. Belief that goodness and love can prevail, and that the world can be a better place. We need to believe that this is possible, that we can make it so .... because knowing our frailties as men and women we need to believe that there is something larger and better than ourselves, a God, who will give us the strength to do this.'

Yes, possibly we do?

But then, and don't ask me why, I asked,

"I wonder what happened to the bat?"

"Didn't you mention the name, Puriel?" Reverend Money asked.

"Yes, I think that is what Teddy had called it," I replied, without thinking why he had asked the question or why it might be relevant.

"Puriel? If my memory serves me well, it is the name of an angel, an angel of judgement, also known as The Fire of God?"

he said with a hint of a smile, possibly at the realisation that we boys weren't quite so ignorant and disinterested in such things as we pretended to be.

Yes, I thought, that is just the sort of thing that Bobby would have known.

"So you don't think it died in the fire?" I asked and then immediately wished I hadn't, as it sounded such a silly, childish thing to say, but I guess I was just so pleased and relieved to have something positive to cling to at last.

Chapter 16

To One Who Has Faith, No Explanation Is Necessary. To One Without Faith, No Explanation Is Possible.

Everyone around the table relaxed and breathed a collective sigh of relief, thinking that Thomas's story was over.

"Wow, Tom. That was certainly some tale," said Dan.

"Is that what really happened? You didn't make that up, did you?" asked young Derek in a voice which suggested a certain amount of doubt as to whether such a strange tale, although sounding too far-fetched to be true, might just in fact be so.

Tom didn't answer and instead replied with,

"The story of those days didn't quite end there. Did I mention that we had to travel to our new school by bus?

This was a bit of a bore because we had to get up earlier in order to catch it; no more last minute getting out of bed and rushing across the field, not that I had done much of that in the previous term, being like all the other boys in having an ulterior motive, that of seeing a shapely Louise Loveless in her partially open blouse, or tight jumper, to get to my class on time! However, one ulterior motive gave way to another, and the new one for me was Marianne Cole.

Marianne and I used to sit next to each other on the bus," continued Tom, "and after a first stolen kiss and cuddle, innocent intimacy became the morning and afternoon joy of the day and was incentive enough for me to get out of bed in the morning! I kidded myself that we even became an 'item,' and remained one for the next two terms until suddenly everything unravelled in the following summer holidays.

I had called in at her house, and she and I were sitting in the garden being very grown up, whilst her mother was in the kitchen preparing their evening meal, and no doubt keeping an eye on us. Suddenly, Marianne jumped up and said,

"Would you like to see something?"

Well, I was a hot-blooded teenager back then, and so of course my speculation as to what she meant by 'Would you like to see something?' went way off the radar, and I stood up to follow her.

"No. You wait here," she commanded, as if she had second-guessed what I was thinking.

With my fanciful thoughts doused in iced water, I slumped back down in the deck chair and started to wonder what on earth it was she wanted to show me. A couple of minutes later, she bounced back on to the patio with something wrapped in an old towel.

"Do you know what this is?"

As I honestly hadn't got the faintest idea and was still suffering from the 'cold shower', I came out with a somewhat unenthusiastic,

"No."

"Well if you don't want to see it ...."

"OK, go on. What is it?"

"Bet you'll never guess."

And she was right. I would never have guessed. She sat down next to me and slowly unrolled the towel and there lying in the middle of it was .... the bat!

"Where did you get that?" I asked, feeling the blood draining from my face.

"You know," she said, giving me the same conspiratorial

wink that she had given me in class that day when I had seen her lift the glass bell-jar without Miss Loveless noticing.

I felt as if the bottom had just fallen out of my world. Oh Marianne, you, so obviously, have absolutely no idea what I've heard about that bat! And if you haven't, what about others? Was I the only one who'd heard Teddy's story? And if the bat was here, on that towel ….? Teddy? Teddy, you rotten sod! Were you having me on? Was that just another of your pranks? And if that was so, was the account that I'd subsequently read in the newspaper true after all? The incontrovertible, hard evidence that I now had there, right in front of me, lying in the middle of a towel, was most certainly suggesting that it was.

For two full terms I had taken Teddy's version of events as the truth, and …. Oh no! I'd even spoken at considerable length with our vicar about it, and could feel myself flushing with embarrassment at the recollection. What must he have thought of me? You idiot, Tom! And then I was back full circle, back to wondering what Marianne must have been thinking of me with, what to her, must have been my totally unexpected reaction.

"May I?" I asked, reaching for the very-dead-looking animal.

I turned it over in my hands, and as far as I could see, it looked much the same as I remembered it when I had last seen it in the bell-jar hanging from its piece of tree. Hadn't the other escapees returned to their cases looking 'healthier' than when they had left? This one certainly didn't look 'healthier'. Neither were any scorch marks on its moth-eaten-looking fur and dry leathery wings. I even lifted it up and smelt it. There was just the smell of dusty, musty age and not a hint of either smoke or singed fur, and neither were there any bits of loose dried flesh or blood on its claws. Indeed, there was absolutely nothing to indicate that it had been anywhere near a burning classroom, let alone had been involved in a life and death battle between the forces of good and evil.

Marianne must have thought I'd gone completely mad and

was, I expect, more than a little disappointed at my reaction upon seeing this obviously wonderful treasure. Possibly, she'd thought that we might have had some happy reminiscing as a result of my seeing it. Whereas instead, my seeing that little moth-eaten mammal had completely the opposite effect on me. I sat there as if I had seen a ghost and feeling a complete and utter fool. Well, as you can probably guess, that was when our relationship started to go downhill, as I couldn't find it in myself to explain how I'd been taken-in with Teddy's account, and without this explanation she couldn't possibly understand my reaction upon seeing the bat again. 'The course of true love never did run smooth.'[27]

It was probably after seeing that very dead-looking, stuffed bat of Marianne's that I started to really question what it was that I had actually witnessed, to ask myself, what, of this whole saga, had I actually seen with my own eyes, and I began to realise that possibly, I'd seen very little. I'd only got Teddy's word that Renard the fox had left his case, as I had never seen the case empty. And what about his rejuvenated snout? Had it actually changed, or were our imaginations all so hyped-up that we were convinced it had, and so reinforced each other's opinions that this was so? Yes, I had paid a nocturnal visit to a classroom bathed in intermittent moonlight and, with my heart in my mouth and with a very susceptible imagination which had probably been working overtime at the time, had seen that a ring had somehow materialised in a case containing a stuffed magpie. But had the magpie actually left the case, as we were all probably wanting to believe, taken the ring and returned with it? Or was there, as Reverend Money had suggested, another explanation? It was, after all, Teddy who had found that particular exhibit, so had he slipped the ring into the case before calling Bobby and myself over? Had this been just another of his pranks? And was his subsequent suggestion that it had better be left there, nothing whatsoever to do with the Thompsons

---

[27] William Shakespeare, A Midsummer Night's Dream (Act 1, Scene 1).

being likely to be blamed for the ring being there, and far more to do with extending the prank, so that not only did it take me in, but also took in the whole school? In which case, I could be certain that Bobby was also in on it, because if this was a prank, it sounded as if it was just a little too well thought through to be just Teddy's idea, and of course, this would explain why he and Bobby had found it so hard to keep straight faces during the Reverend Bitterling's exorcism.

And when did Marianne remove the bat from the bell-jar? Yes, I should have asked her, but after that day when she showed it to me, I just couldn't bring myself to even mention the bat to her again. She must have taken it of course, as I was absolutely certain that 'her bat' that I saw wrapped in the towel was one-and-the-same-bat as the one I had seen in the bell-jar. With hindsight it was obvious that she would have said nothing during this period, and no doubt she was probably only too relieved that various rumours about the bat were doing the rounds, as all knew she liked things ghoulish and so she would have known that she would be suspected of its disappearance, and so anything which took attention away from her must have been welcome. The subsequent breaking of the bat's bell-jar during Bitterling's exorcism, of course left her, with her newly acquired treasure, nicely in the clear.

What other 'hard facts' were there? I racked my brains, but couldn't think of any, and thus, it suddenly became very apparent that all the facts that I had thought looked so 'hard' just a few months previously, now didn't look in the least bit 'hard'. Indeed, they didn't even look like facts at all! Reverend Money's words came somewhat embarrassingly back to me, 'I am not for a moment saying that the version of events that you have told me is not true, I am just suggesting that we should be careful not to jump to conclusions. At this point in time we don't know all the facts, and so there may be other explanations for what has happened and so we do need to keep open minds on this.' Oh dear. Had I been only too willing to just accept without question any 'truth' that had been presented to me?

So were the Reverend Bitterling's and Aidan's deaths just coincidental? When I then thought about it, the only thing that linked these to Louise Loveless was coincidence; that of having occurred closely after the disappearance of the bat from its bell-jar and the subsequent breaking of the jar at Reverend Bitterling's exorcism, though at that stage, all blame was being heaped on the bat, not on Louise Loveless. It was only later, after the fire at the school, that blame was suddenly shifted from the bat to her. So in 'hard factual terms' there was absolutely nothing to link these two deaths to anything or anyone. So that left me with Teddy's account of the fire at the school and the newspaper account of the same. Which was true? I honestly didn't know, even though I had supposedly witnessed most of the story! What was the truth of what had happened?

And so belatedly, it hit me that I had no real hard facts which proved anything. All the so-called 'evidence' that I had was that which I'd thought I'd seen, that which I'd thought had been so, that which I'd heard from others, that which I'd believed to be the case. So does this mean that the truth of anything is what one believes it to be, simply because one believes it to be so?

Then for some reason, Felicity's words came back to me, 'But religion is *not* about proof, it is about belief.' Her quotation from Hebrews, 'Faith is the substance of things hoped for, the evidence of things not seen,'[28] said much the same thing, though in a more poetic manner. And Reverend Money had said much the same when he'd explained, 'If you believe, Tom, you do, and no explanation is necessary. However, if you don't, then you don't. You can't prove God.' But I wasn't trying to 'prove God'! I was just trying to ascertain the truth of a series of incidents which I thought I had witnessed."

At this point, Tom paused for a moment, collected his

---

[28] Hebrews 11:1

thoughts and then continued,

"However, all the foregoing happened something like fifty years ago. What is just as strange and much more disconcerting is what happened only a couple of days ago, which brings us back to our earlier conversation of this evening, the one which prompted this story."

He paused again and looked round the table; was it to ensure that he had our attention?

"You see, Samantha and I are going to be away on the collection day for the clothes for the Air Ambulance. We're off to Tenerife for some sun. So I'd been sent down to the church with two bin-liners full of clothes to drop them off somewhere. I had no idea where, but fortunately ran into our new young vicar, the Reverend Green, coming out of the church, and so asked him if he knew where I should leave the bags. Although I say *our* new young vicar, it seems from what he told me, as if our village will be sharing him with something like three others, which means that he won't be exclusively *ours,* as he'll only be here on about one Sunday a month.

It's interesting to note how people's need to believe and worship has changed over the years. Is this as a result of education, as a young Bobby Thompson had pointed out all those years ago, - when you know how the planets in our solar system revolve around the sun, then the sun rising every morning doesn't appear so magical, or so ordained by a god, - and so hence does the need to believe diminish? Perhaps a somewhat simplistic assumption, because most of us don't really understand planetary motion and have to take the astronomers' and scientists' word for it. In which case, have we not just shifted our belief from a belief in a God or gods to a belief in astronomers and scientists; a shift from believing in the spiritual to believing in the temporal? Or does our need to believe change with wealth and standard of living? The poor are more conscious of hard times, bad luck, etc., and so inevitably have a greater need of some form of moral support, something to hold onto when they are down, as my old teacher, Felicity, might have said. Whereas when we have a good job, good money, a nice house, a nice car and food on the table, does our need for hope and belief in something greater than ourselves decline because we feel economically and physically safer in our lives? But in spite of this, how many of us still 'touch wood' and 'cross fingers', and, when something more serious impacts on our lives, decide that we will 'pray for'? Where is our faith in science then? So is our need to believe just as strong as ever, and our denial of it just arrogant vanity and hubris?

Anyway, my musings aside," said Tom, adopting a lighter tone, "our new vicar and I had a bit of a chat, during which he asked me how long I'd lived in the village and then, as I mentioned at the start of this evening, asked if I'd attended the old school. I explained to him that there had been two old schools; the one opposite the church which is now a tearoom, and the other one, which used to be in the field as you come into the village, the one I've just been telling you about. Upon hearing this Reverend Green went strangely quiet.

"Is there something wrong?" I asked.

"Er, no, no," he replied in a manner which clearly indicated that something *was* wrong.

After a brief pause, he then, somewhat hesitantly asked,

"Did you know one of my predecessors, the Reverend Money?"

"Oh yes." I replied. "He was the vicar here when I was a bairn (child). I remember him well. A nice chap, one of the few vicars I've been able to get on with. Sorry, no offence intended, but we've had some odd ones over the years. Bitterling, he was the one before Money, he was a strange one. The poor man died right in front of the altar in this very church. It was an odd business, frightened the life out of everyone in the village as you can probably imagine. Reverend Money was his curate at the time and then took over as our vicar, but that was something like forty to fifty years ago."

"Yes, yes, I know," he said, still preoccupied with whatever it was that had struck him when I'd mentioned the old school.

"Perhaps you could help me?" he asked.

What was it that had so obviously troubled him when I'd mentioned the old school, and how did he think I was going to be able to help him? In spite of my having no idea, I replied,

"If I can."

"We can leave these here," he said, indicating the two plastic bags full of old clothes that I held and the bench in the church porch in which we were standing. After I'd put them down, he and I went into the building proper. He set off down the nave to the small vestry, and I followed him.

"Come in", he said over his shoulder and then bade me sit down.

He retired behind a desk, opened a cupboard on the far wall and took out an old wooden box, placed it on the desk and opened it. The box was, of course, facing him, and its raised hinged lid hid its contents from my view. He then took out a piece of folded paper and handed it to me. On it was written in what I then saw was the Reverend Money's unmistakable hand,

'Lest I forget why I am here.'

Beneath this was:-

'(found in field, adjacent to school)'

and this was followed by a date which I recognised immediately. And it was then that the weight of what was written on that piece of paper hit me. 'Oh Goodness! What has come back to haunt me after all this time?' And an unpleasant chill started to creep over me.

"May I ask what is in the box?" I said, knowing that I had to ask, but wishing that I did not.

The Reverend Green slowly turned the box round in a slightly theatrical manner using just the tips of his fingers, which I took as suggesting that he wanted nothing to do with its contents.

"Oh no!" I found myself saying out loud as the jumbled events of fifty years previously come flooding back like an ice-cold tidal wave!

Inside the box was a badly fire-damaged silver chalice. Even though I had never seen it before, there was no mistaking what it was. The pentagram (an upside down five pointed star) engraved on it, left no doubt about *that*. It was most certainly not for Church use. So it was this, and the fact that Reverend Money had kept it that had been preoccupying our Reverend Green, and had caused all his earlier hesitation.

"Do you think the Reverend Money ....?" he asked.

"Oh goodness me, no. He was one of the good guys," I said quickly and somewhat nervously, as I was, at the same time, frantically trying to reassess the events of fifty years earlier in the bright new light of what I was now looking at.

"Does the date mean anything to you?" He asked in a lighter tone, obviously relieved at my having set his mind at ease about Reverend Money.

"Yes. It's two days after the school burnt down.

And .... er .... was there anything else?"

Anything like a large knife, a Lucifarian Athame, I think they are called, by any chance? But, of course, I didn't voice these thoughts as I was desperately hoping that it wasn't there, desperately hoping that the story Teddy had told me so many years previously was not true.

"No, this was all. Were you expecting something else?"

"Um .... I, I just wondered," I mumbled, as I realised that the fact that the knife had not been found by Reverend Money did not invalidate Teddy's story. Indeed, the very fact that our then-vicar had found the chalice in the field, all but confirmed it.

Possibly the police had found the knife, the murder weapon, and simply had not looked for the chalice, which was why Reverend Money had been able to find it? But if that was so, why had the story of Loveless being a heroine and her attempting to rescue young what-was-her-name printed in the newspaper? To the best of my knowledge, there had been no mention of any knife. So if it had existed, what had happened to it?

"Do you have any idea how he came by this?" Reverend Green asked.

"Oh yes," I replied absently, because my thoughts and memories were, right then, of a flame ravaged burning classroom, of that night fifty years ago, when a usually irrepressible Teddy, had been sobbing and shaking in an oversized coat and had told me the most bizarre and insane story. A story of a demented Louise Loveless dressed in a blood soaked semi-transparent white surplice, with horns on her head, looking like some mad she-devil, flailing wildly at the air with a huge knife and then madly hacking at something on the floor of the room!

Oh goodness! What was her name? .... Sheila .... Yes, Sheila Simonds. Oh dear! That poor girl!

And yes, memories of a bat, a small black leathery bat, which we had all so misunderstood, also in that same blazing room effortlessly avoiding the blade aimed at it, fearlessly swooping and diving at the deranged Loveless until it had eventually struck what was to be the mortal blow, which had sent her out of balance, over her makeshift altar and into the waiting inferno.

And on that makeshift altar to evil had been a lit candle

and .... and *that* chalice!

But the other version of events was simultaneously churning in my head; the newspaper version. The version which had described Louise Loveless as the selfless heroine who'd died attempting to save poor Sheila Simonds from the burning building. The version which also had the bat, which Marianne had showed me wrapped up in an old towel, which I could have sworn was the very same bat that I had seen in the bell-jar and that most certainly had been nowhere near any form of fire, and so couldn't possibly have been in a burning classroom.

And just as I had noted all those years ago, all the 'evidence' seemed so totally contradictory with none of it hanging together to point to any definitive truth.

"Well actually, no," I continued hesitantly, "as I have no idea what is and what is not true."

There was an odd sort of silence between us, with myself wondering how I was going to explain my contradictory answer, and he no doubt wondering why I had given him such an odd response.

Which of the two histories was true? What was the truth of this? I hadn't been able to answer that back then, and I still couldn't just a couple of days ago. And strangely, after all those intervening years I was again back to realising that it was not just these two histories that had a 'truth problem'. What about all histories, or all history? 'What is history, but a fable agreed upon.'[29] What can we trust as being one hundred percent true, because doesn't that very much depend on who wrote it, usually the winner, and precisely what evidence they had managed/wished to ascertain/had access to? And what about religion? What about the existence or otherwise of God? And which, if any, of all the religions, including the various versions of them, and that which I had read about in that newspaper back

---

[29] Attributed to Napoleon.

when I was a schoolboy, were true? What is true? Is there any truth to anything? Indeed, what is Truth? Is it simply what one believes it to be? Are all the stories of our lives, all our histories, indeed is all history, what we believe it to be; which may, or may not be, as it actually was? In which case, if what we believe something to have been, or believe it to be, is so closely linked to what actually was and/or is, then is 'belief' as valid as 'fact' and visa-versa? Are both just different forms of 'truth' and so equally valid?"

But why can't this be a little more simple, a little more straightforward? Why do all the facts, does all the evidence have to be so contradictory and so inconclusive? I found myself sympathising with the French philosopher, Michel de Montaigne, who famously had said, 'Que sais-je' ('What know I?'), and I confess felt a degree of relief at realising that others far more learned than I, had also had problems with analysing truth. Indeed, I very nearly quoted de Montaigne to our new vicar, but oddly, oddly because I hadn't expected it, Reverend Money's words came back to me, so instead I found myself saying,

"'To one who has faith, no explanation is necessary. To one without faith, no explanation is possible.'" Not because this quotation gave any definitive answer, but probably because it simply states how things are.

"That sounds like St Thomas Aquinas," said Reverend Green brightly.

"Yes, probably," I replied, less enthusiastically. "Reverend Money used to like to quote him. But," I continued, "as to your earlier question regarding how this - would you describe it as a chalice? - comes to be here, no, I'm not at all sure, but if you have an hour or two."

There was a gentle chuckle from everyone sitting around the table, as thus, Tom concluded his tale.

"I am a little surprised that Reverend Money didn't take that chalice with him when he moved on," remarked Verity. "He wouldn't have written that little - what was it? - 'Lest I forget ....'"

"'.... why I am here,'" added Tom.

"Yes. He wouldn't have written that without good reason and also if it didn't mean something to him."

"Yes, that and the chalice's very existence is what is so very disconcerting. But, as regards his leaving it, didn't he have to take up his next appointment in a bit of a hurry, and so possibly, forgot it? The chalice, that is, not his reason for keeping it." suggested Tom.

"Do you think it is still at the church?" asked Helen.

"I don't know," Tom replied, "and I have no idea if Marianne Cole, still has that stuffed bat, though I suspect not. However, as regards the chalice, I got the feeling that our Reverend Green would probably prefer that such a thing wasn't kept in the church, and so I suspect he has probably already forwarded it on to the Bishop, or Reverend Money, if he knows where he is these days."

"So what do you think happened, Tom?" asked Brian.

"Honestly, I have no idea. Which 'truth' do you wish to belief?"

END

And did you enjoy this story?

If you did, could you be so kind as to post a review (it need only be three or four words), or just your star rating, on any or all of:-

Amazon.com, amazon.co.uk Goodreads and Bookbub or any other platform you choose.

Thank you. And as a favour for yourself? Well, now you know what my stories are like; possibly try another one?

Thank you for reading.

More information can be found on my website, and you can follow me on social media, via
https://www.linktr.ee/lesliegarland

<u>Acknowledgements</u>

Although this tale is a work of fiction, a work of my imagination, nonetheless many have both wittingly and unwittingly contributed to it. So to all of them, I am much obliged to you for providing me with material, ideas, snippets, etc., all of which are necessary for the writing of a story. My gratitude is also posthumously due to Aud, my late wife, who provided me with the necessary space to write, the much needed words of encouragement along the way and for proofreading the final original manuscript. I must also not forget all the advance readers who have taken the time to read my work and post their oh-so-necessary reviews and words of encouragement; thank you all. And finally I must thank the team at Noble Legacy Publishing for their editorial ideas, behind the scenes efforts and the superb cover picture.

About the Author

Leslie Garland is the author of The Red Grouse Tales series. His stories blend history, faith, and supernatural suspense, exploring the mysteries of belief, temptation, and ancient evil. They have been both Book Excellence Awards Finalists and achieved Readers' Favorite 5-star status.

He lives in Northumberland, England, UK., is inspired by folklore and the landscapes around him and is currently working on various new tales.

<u>Also by Leslie Garland:-</u>

- The Little Dog

- The Crow

- The Golden Tup

- The White Hart

- The Red Grouse Tales: The Little Dog and other stories.

- The Ghost Moth

- The Blue Horse

Visit **www.lesliegarland.com** for further information

Published in Collaboration with Noble Legacy Publishing
<u>www.noblelegacypublishing.co.uk</u>

www.ingramcontent.com/pod-product-compliance
Lightning Source LLC
Chambersburg PA
CBHW040228170726

48295CB00014B/841